YOUNG PEOPLE'S PRIDE

A NOVEL

STEPHEN VINCENT BENET

Young People's Pride

Stephen Vincent Benet

© 1st World Library, 2006
PO Box 2211
Fairfield, IA 52556
www.1stworldlibrary.com
First Edition

LCCN: 2006936243

Softcover ISBN: 978-1-4218-3106-0
Hardcover ISBN: 978-1-4218-3006-3
eBook ISBN: 978-1-4218-3206-7

Purchase *"Young People's Pride"*
as a traditional bound book at:
www.1stWorldLibrary.com/purchase.asp?ISBN=978-1-4218-3106-0

1st World Library is a literary, educational organization
dedicated to:

- Creating a free internet library of downloadable ebooks

- Hosting writing competitions and offering book
publishing scholarships.

Interested in more 1st World Library books?
contact: literacy@1stworldlibrary.com
Check us out at: www.1stworldlibrary.com

1ˢᵗ World Library Literary Society

Giving Back to the World

"If you want to work on the core problem, it's early school literacy."

- James Barksdale, former CEO of Netscape

"No skill is more crucial to the future of a child, or to a democratic and prosperous society, than literacy."

- Los Angeles Times

Literacy... means far more than learning how to read and write... The aim is to transmit... knowledge and promote social participation."

- UNESCO

"Literacy is not a luxury, it is a right and a responsibility. If our world is to meet the challenges of the twenty-first century we must harness the energy and creativity of all our citizens."

- President Bill Clinton

"Parents should be encouraged to read to their children, and teachers should be equipped with all available techniques for teaching literacy, so the varying needs and capacities of individual kids can be taken into account."

- Hugh Mackay

TO ROSEMARY

If I were sly, I'd steal for you that cobbled hill, Montmartre,
Josephine's embroidered shoes, St. Louis' oriflamme,
The river on grey evenings and the bluebell-glass of Chartes,
And four sarcastic gargoyles from the roof of Notre Dame.

That wouldn't be enough, though, enough nor half a part;
There'd be shells because they're sorrowful, and pansies since
they're wise,
The smell of rain on lilac-bloom, less fragrant than your heart,
And that small blossom of your name, as steadfast as your eyes.

Sapphires, pirates, sandalwood, porcelains, sonnets, pearls,
Sunsets gay as Joseph's coat and seas like milky jade,
Dancing at your birthday like a mermaid's dancing curls
—If my father'd only brought me up to half a decent trade!

Nothing I can give you—nothing but the rhymes—
Nothing but the empty speech, the idle words and few,
The mind made sick with irony you helped so many times,
The strengthless water of the soul your truthfulness kept true.

Take the little withered things and neither laugh nor cry
—Gifts to make a sick man glad he's going out like sand—
They and I are yours, you know, as long as there's an I.
Take them for the ages. Then they may not shame your hand.

"... For there groweth in great abundance in this land a small flower, much blown about by winds, named 'Young People's Pride'..."

DYCER'S *Herbal*

YOUNG PEOPLES PRIDE

I

It is one of Johnny Chipman's parties at the Harlequin Club, and as usual the people the other people have been asked to meet are late and as usual Johnny is looking hesitatingly around at those already collected with the nervous kindliness of an absent-minded menagerie-trainer who is trying to make a happy family out of a wombat, a porcupine, and two small Scotch terriers because they are all very nice and he likes them all and he can't quite remember at the moment just where he got hold of any of them. This evening he has been making an omelet of youngest. K. Ricky French, the youngest Harvard playwright to learn the tricks of C43, a Boston exquisite, impeccably correct from his club tie to the small gold animal on his watch-chain, is almost coming to blows with Slade Wilson, the youngest San Francisco cartoonist to be tempted East by a big paper and still so new to New York that no matter where he tries to take the subway, he always finds himself buried under Times Square, over a question as to whether La Perouse or Foyot's has the best *hors-d'oeuvres* in Paris.

The conflict is taking place across Johnny's knees, both of which are being used for emphasis by the disputants till he is nearly mashed like a sandwich-filling between two argumentative slices of bread, but he is quite content. Peter Piper, the youngest rare-book collector in the country, who, if left to himself, would have gravitated naturally toward French and a devastating conversation in monosyllables on the pretty failings of prominent debutantes, is gradually warming Clark Stovall, the youngest star of the Provincetown Players out of a prickly silence, employed in supercilious blinks at all the large pictures of celebrated Harlequins by discreet, intelligent questions as to the probable future of Eugene O'Neill.

Stovall has just about decided to throw Greenwich Village omniscience overboard and admit privately to himself that people like Peter can be both human and interesting even if they do live in the East Sixties instead of Macdougal Alley when a page comes in discreetly for Johnny Chipman. Johnny rises like an agitated blond robin who has just spied the very two worms he was keeping room for to top off breakfast. "Well" he says to the world at large. "They're only fifteen minutes late apiece this time."

He darts out into the hall and reappears in a moment, a worm on either side. Both worms will fit in easily with the youthful assortment already gathered—neither can be more than twenty-five.

Oliver Crowe is nearly six feet, vividly dark, a little stooping, dressed like anybody else in the Yale Club from hair parted in the middle to low heavyish brown shoes, though the punctured patterns on the latter are a year or so out of date. There is very little that is remarkable about his appearance except the round, rather large head that shows writer or pugilist indifferently, brilliant eyes, black as black warm marble under heavy tortoise-shell glasses and a mouth that is not weak in the least but somehow burdened by a pressure upon it like a pressure of wings, the pressure of that kind of dream which will not release the flesh it inhabits always and agonizes often until it is given perfect body and so does not release it until such flesh has ceased. At present he is not the youngest anything, except, according to himself 'the youngest failure in advertising,' but a book of nakedly youthful love-poetry, which in gloomy moments he wishes had never been written, although the *San Francisco Warbler* called it as 'tensely vital as the Shropshire Lad,' brought him several column reviews and very nearly forty dollars in cash at twenty-one and since then many people of his own age and one or two editors have considered him "worth watching."

Ted Billett is dark too, but it is a ruddy darkness with high clear color of skin. He could pass anywhere as a College Senior and though his clothes seem to have been put on anyhow with no regard for pressing or tailoring they will always raise a doubt in the minds of the uninstructed as to whether it is not the higher carelessness that has dictated them rather than ordinary poverty—a doubt that, in many cases, has proved innocently fortunate for Ted. His hands are a curious mixture of square executive ability and imaginative sensitiveness and his surface manners have often been described as 'too snotty' by delicate souls toward whom Ted was entirely unconscious of having acted with anything but the most disinterested politeness. On the other hand a certain even-tempered recklessness and capacity for putting himself in the other fellow's place made him one of the few popularly lenient officers to be obeyed with discipline in his outfit during the war. As regards anything Arty or Crafty his attitude is merely appreciative—he is finishing up his last year of law at Columbia.

Johnny introduces Oliver and Ted to everybody but Peter—the three were classmates—shepherds his flock with a few disarmingly personal insults to prevent stiffness closing down again over the four that have already got to talking at the arrival of the two newcomers, and marshals them out to the terrace where they are to have dinner. Without seeming to try, he seats them so that Ted, Peter and Oliver will not form an offensive-defensive alliance against the three who are strangers to them by retailing New Haven anecdotes to each other for the puzzlement of the rest and starts the ball rolling with a neat provocative attack on romanticism in general and Cabell in particular.

II

"Johnny's strong for realism, aren't you, Johnny?"

"Well, yes, Ted, I am. I think 'Main Street' and 'Three Soldiers' are two of the best things that ever happened to America. You can say it's propaganda—maybe it is, but at any rate it's real. Honestly, I've gotten so tired, we all have, of all this stuff about the small Middle Western Town being the backbone of the country—"

"Backbone? Last vertebra!"

"As for 'Main Street,' it's—"

"It's the hardest book to read through without fallin' asleep where you sit, though, that I've struck since the time I had to repeat Geology." Peter smiles. "But, there, Johnny, I guess I'm the bone-head part of the readin' public—"

"That's why you're just the kind of person that ought to read books like that, Peter. The reading public in general likes candy laxatives, I'll admit—Old Nest stuff—but you—"

"Nobody else will ever have to write the description of a small Middle Western Town" quotes Oliver, discontentedly. "Well, who ever wanted to write the description of a small Middle Western Town?" and from Ricky French, selecting his words like flowers for a *boutonniere*.

"The trouble with 'Main Street' is not that it isn't the truth but that it isn't nearly the whole truth. Now Sherwood Anderson—"

"Tennyson. Who *was* Tennyson? He died young."

"Well, if *that* is Clara Stratton's idea of how to play a woman who did."

The two sentences seem to come from no one and arrive nowhere. They are batted out of the conversation like toy balloons.

"Bunny Andrews sailed for Paris Thursday," says Ted Billett longingly. "Two years at the Beaux Arts," and for an instant the splintering of lances stops, like the hush in a tournament when the marshal throws down the warder, at the shine of that single word.

"All the same, New York is the best place to be right now if you're going to do anything big," says Johnny uncomfortably, too much as if he felt he just had to believe in it, but the rest are silent, seeing the Seine wind under its bridges, cool as satin, grey-blue with evening, or the sawdust of a restaurant near the quais where one can eat Rabelaisiantly for six francs with wine and talk about anything at all without having to pose or explain or be defensive, or the chimneypots of La Cite branch-black against winter sky that is pallor of crimson when the smell of roast chestnuts drifts idly as a student along Boulevard St. Germain, or none of these, or all, but for each one nostalgic aspect of the city where good Americans go when they die and bad ones while they live—to Montmartre.

"New York *is* twice as romantic, really," says Johnny firmly.

"If you can't get out of it," adds Oliver with a twisted grin.

Ted Billett turns to Ricky French as if each had no other friend in the world.

"You were over, weren't you?" he says, a little diffidently, but his voice is that of Rachel weeping for her children.

"Well, there was a little cafe on the Rue Bonaparte—I suppose you wouldn't know—"

III

The party has adjourned to Stovall's dog-kennel-sized apartment on West Eleventh Street with oranges and ice, Peter Piper having suddenly remembered a little place he knows where what gin is to be bought is neither diluted Croton water nor hell-fire. The long drinks gather pleasantly on the table, are consumed by all but Johnny, gather again. The talk grows more fluid, franker.

"Phil Sellaby?—-oh, the great Phil's just had a child—I mean his wife has, but Phil's been having a book all winter and it's hard not to get 'em mixed up. Know the girl he married?"

"Ran Waldo had a necking acquaintance with her at one time or another, I believe. But now she's turned serious, I hear—*tres serieuse—tres bonne femme*—"

"I bet his book'll be a cuckoo, then. Trouble with women. Can't do any art and be married if you're in love with your wife. Instink—instinct of creation—same thing in both cases—use it one way, not enough left for other—unless, of course, like Goethe, you—" "Rats! Look at Rossetti—Browning—-Augustus John—William Morris—"

"*Browning!* Dear man, when the public knows the *truth* about the Brownings!"

Ricky French is getting a little drunk but it shows itself only in a desire to make every sentence unearthly cogent with perfect words.

"Unhappy marriage—ver' good—stimula-shion," he says, carefully but unsteadily, "other thing—tosh!"

Peter Piper jerks a thumb in Oliver's direction.

"Oh, beg pardon! Engaged, you told me? Beg pardon—sorry—very. Writes?"

"Uh-huh. Book of poetry three years ago. Novel now he's trying to sell."

"Oh, yes, yes, yes. Remember. 'Dancers' Holiday'—he wrote that? Good stuff, damn good. Too bad. Feenee. Why will they get married?"

The conversation veers toward a mortuary discussion of love. Being young, nearly all of them are anxious for, completely puzzled by and rather afraid of it, all at the same time. They wish to draw up one logical code to cover its every variation; they look at it, as it is at present with the surprised displeasure of florists at a hollyhock that will come blue when by every law of variation it should be rose. It is only a good deal later that they will be able to give, not blasphemy because the rules of the game are always mutually inconsistent, but tempered thanks that there are any rules at all. Now Ricky French especially has the air of a demonstrating anatomist over an anesthetized body. "Observe, gentlemen—the carotid artery lies here. Now, inserting the scalpel at this point—"

"The trouble with Art is that it doesn't pay a decent living wage unless you're willing to commercialize—"

"The trouble with Art is that it never did, except for a few chance lucky people—"

"The trouble with Art is women."

"The trouble with women is Art."

"The trouble with Art—with women, I mean—change signals! What do I mean?"

IV

Oliver is taking Ted out to Melgrove with him over Sunday for suburban fresh-air and swimming, so the two just manage to catch the 12.53 from the Grand Central, in spite of Slade Wilson's invitation to talk all night and breakfast at the Brevoort. They spend the rattling, tunnel-like passage to 125th Street catching their breath again, a breath that seems to strike a florid gentlemen in a dirty collar ahead of them with an expression of permanent, sorrowful hunger. Then Ted remarks reflectively,

"Nice gin."

"Uh-huh. Not floor varnish anyway like most of this prohibition stuff. What think of the people?"

"Interesting but hardly conclusive. Liked the Wilson lad. Peter, of course, and Johnny. The French person rather young Back Bay, don't you think?"

Oliver smiles. The two have been through Yale, some of the war and much of the peace together, and the fact has inevitably developed a certain quality of being able to talk to each other in shorthand.

"Well, Groton plus Harvard—it always gets a little inhuman especially Senior year—but gin had a civilizing influence. Lucky devil!"

Stephen Vincent Benet

"Why?"

"Baker's newest discovery—yes, it does sound like a patent medicine. Don't mean that, but he has a play on the road—sure-fire, Johnny says—Edward Sheldon stuff—Romance—"

"The Young Harvard Romantic. An Essay Presented to the Faculty of Yale University by Theodore Billett for the Degree of—"

"Heard anything about your novel, Oliver?"

"Going to see my pet Mammon of Unrighteousness about it in a couple of weeks. Oh *Lord!*"

"Present—not voting."

"Don't be cheap, Ted. If I could only make some money."

"Everybody says that there is money in advertising," Ted quotes maliciously. "Where *have* I heard that before?"

"That's what anybody says about anything till they try it. Well, there is—but not in six months for a copy-writer at Vanamee and Co. Especially when the said copy-writer has to have enough to marry on." "And will write novels when he ought to be reading, 'How I Sold America on Ossified Oats' like a good little boy. Young people are *so* impatient."

"Well, good Lord, Ted, we've been engaged eight months already and we aren't getting any furtherer—"

"Remember the copybooks, my son. The love of a pure, good woman and the one-way pocket—that's what makes the millionaires. Besides, look at Isaac."

"Well, I'm no Isaac. And Nancy isn't Rebekah, praises be! But it is an—emotional strain. On both of us."

"Well, all you have to do is sell your serial rights. After that—pie."

"I know. The trouble is, I can see it so plain if everything happens right—and then—well—"

Ted is not very consoling.

"People get funny ideas about each other when they aren't close by. Even when they're in love," he says rather darkly; and then, for no apparent reason, "Poor Billy. See it?"

Oliver has, unfortunately—the announcement that the engagement between Miss Flavia Marston of Detroit and Mr. William Curting of New York has been broken by mutual consent was an inconspicuous little paragraph in the morning papers. "That was all—just funny ideas and being away. And then this homebred talent came along," Ted muses.

"Well, you're the hell of a—"

Ted suddenly jerks into consciousness of what he has been saying.

"Sorry" he says, completely apologetic, "didn't mean a word I said, just sorry for Billy, poor guy. 'Fraid it'll break him up pretty bad at first." This seems to make matters rather worse and he changes the subject abruptly. "How's Nancy?" he asks with what he hopes seems disconnected indifference.

"Nancy? All right. Hates St. Louis, of course."

"Should think she might, this summer. Pretty hot there, isn't it?"

"Says it's like a wet furnace. And her family's bothering her some."

"Um, too bad."

"Oh, *I* don't mind. But it's rotten for her. They don't see the point exactly—don't know that I blame them. She could be in Paris, now—that woman was ready to put up the money. My fault."

"Well, she seems to like things better the way they are—God knows why, my antic friend! If it were *my* question between you and a year studying abroad! Not that you haven't your own subtle attractions, Ollie." Ted has hoped to irritate Oliver into argument by the closing remark, but the latter only accepts it with militant gloom.

"Yes, I've done her out of that, too," he says abysmally, "as well as sticking her in St. Louis while I stay here and can't even drag down enough money to support her—"

"Oh, Ollie, snap out of it! That's only being dramatic. You know darn well you will darn soon. I'll be saying 'bless you, my children, increase and multiply,' inside a month if your novel goes through."

"If! Oh well. Oh hell. I think I've wept on your shoulder long enough for tonight, Ted. Tell me your end of it—things breaking all right?"

Ted's face sets into lines that seem curiously foreign and aged for the smooth surface.

"Well—you know my trouble," he brings out at last with some difficulty. "You ought to, anyhow—we've talked each other over too much when we were both rather planko for you not to. I'm getting along, I think. The work—*ca marche assez bien.* And the restlessness—can be stood. That's about all there is to say."

Both are completely serious now.

"Bon. Very glad," says Oliver in a low voice.

"I can stand it. I was awful afraid I couldn't when I first got back. And law interests me, really, though I've lost three years because of the war. And I'm working like a pious little devil with a new assortment of damned and when you haven't any money you can't go on parties in New York unless you raise gravy riding to a fine art. Only sometimes—well, you know how it is—"

Oliver nods.

"I'll be sitting there, at night especially, in that little tin Tophet of a room on Madison Avenue, working. I *can* work, if I do say it myself—I'm hoping to get through with school in January, now. But it gets pretty lonely, sometimes when there's nobody to run into that you can really talk to—the people I used to play with in College are out of New York for the summer— even Peter's down at Southampton most of the time or out at Star Bay—you're in Melgrove—Sam Woodward's married and working in Chicago—Brick Turner's in New Mexico—I've dropped out of the Wall Street bunch in the class that hang out at the Yale Club—I'm posted there anyhow, and besides they've all made money and I haven't, and all they want to talk about is puts and calls. And then you remember things.

"The time my pilot and I blew into Paris when we thought we were hitting somewhere around Nancy till we saw that blessed Eiffel Tower poking out of the fog. And the Hotel de Turenne on Rue Vavin and getting up in the morning and going out for a cafe cognac breakfast, and everything being amiable and pleasant, and kidding along all the dear little ladies that sat on the *terrasse* when they dropped in to talk over last evening's affairs. I suppose I'm a sensualist—"

"Everybody is." from Oliver.

"Well, that's another thing. Women. And love. Ollie, my son, you don't know how very damn lucky you are!"

"I think I do, rather," says Oliver, a little stiffly.

"You don't. Because I'd give everything I have for what you've got and all you can do is worry about whether you'll get married in six months or eight."

"I'm worrying about whether I'll ever get married at all," from Oliver, rebelliously.

"True enough, which is where I'm glowingly sympathetic for you, though you may not notice it. But you're one of the few people I know—officers at least—who came out of the war without stepping all through their American home ideas of morality like a clown through a fake glass window. And I'm—Freuded—if I see how or why you did."

"Don't myself—unless you call it pure accident" says Oliver, frankly. "Well, that's it—women. Don't think I'm in love but the other thing pulls pretty strong. And I want to get married all right, but what girls I know and like best are in Peter's crowd and most of them own their own Rolls Royces—and I won't be earning even a starvation wage for two, inside of three or four years, I suppose. And as you can't get away from seeing and talking to women unless you go and live in a cave—well, about once every two weeks or oftener I'd like to chuck every lawbook I have out of the window on the head of the nearest cop—go across again and get some sort of a worthless job—I speak good enough French to do it if I wanted—and go to hell like a gentleman without having to worry about it any longer. And I won't do that because I'm through with it and the other thing is worth while. So there you are."

"So you don't think you're in love—eh Monsieur Billett?" Oliver puts irritatingly careful quotation marks around the verb. Ted twists a little.

"It all seems so blamed impossible," he says cryptically.

"Oh, I wouldn't call Elinor Piper *that* exactly." Oliver grins. "Even if she is Peter's sister. Old Peter. She's a nice girl."

"*A nice girl?*" Ted begins rather violently. "She's—why she's—" then pauses, seeing the trap.

"Oh very well—that's all I wanted to know."

"Oh don't look so much like a little tin Talleyrand, Ollie! I'm *not* sure—and that's rather more than I'd even hint to anybody else."

"Thanks, little darling." But Ted has been stung too suddenly, even by Oliver's light touch on something which he thought was a complete and mortuary secret, to be in a mood for sarcasm.

"Oh, well, you might as well know. I suppose you do."

"All I know is that you seem to have been visiting—Peter—a good deal this summer."

"Well, it started with Peter."

"It does so often."

"Oh Lord, now I've *got* to tell you. Not that there's anything—definite—to tell." He pauses, looking at his hands.

"Well, I've just been telling you how I feel—sometimes. And other times—being with Elinor—she's been so—kind. But I don't know, Ollie, honestly I don't, and that's that."

"You see," he begins again, "the other thing—Oh, *Lord*, it's so tangled up! But it's just this. It sounds—funny—probably—coming from me—and after France and all that—but I'm not going to—pretend to myself I'm in love with a girl—just because I may—want to get married—the way lots of people do. I can't. And I couldn't with a girl like Elinor anyway—she's too fine."

"She is rather fine," says Oliver appreciatively. "Selective reticence—all that."

"Well, don't you see? And a couple of times—I've been nearly sure. And then something comes and I'm not again—not the way I want to be. And then—Oh, if I were, it wouldn't be much—use—you know—"

"Why not?"

"Well, consider our relative positions—"

"Consider your grandmother's cat! She's a girl—you're a man. She's a lady—you're certainly a gentleman—though that sounds like Jane Austen. And—"

"And she's—well, she isn't the wealthiest young lady in the country, but the Pipers *are* rich, though they never go and splurge around about it. And I'm living on scholarships and borrowed money from the family—and even after I really start working I probably won't make enough to live on for two or three years at least. And you can't ask a girl like that—"

"Oh, Ted, this is the twentieth century! I'm not telling you to hang up your hat and live on your wife's private income—"
"That's fortunate," from Ted, rather stubbornly and with a set jaw.

"But there's no reason on earth—if you both really loved each other and wanted to get married—why you couldn't let her pay her share for the first few years. You know darn well you're going to make money sometime—"

"Well—yes."

"Well, then. And Elinor's sporting. She isn't the kind that needs six butlers to live—she doesn't live that way now. That's just pride, Ted, thinking that—and a rather bum variety of pride when you come down to it. I hate these people who moan around and won't be happy unless they can do everything themselves—they're generally the kind that give their wives a charge account at Lucile's and ten dollars a year pocket money and go into blue fits whenever poor spouse runs fifty cents over her allowance."

Ted pauses, considering. Finally,

"No, Ollie—I don't think I'm quite that kind of a fool. And almost thou convincest me—and all that. But—well—that isn't the chief difficulty, after all."

"Well, what *is?*" from Oliver, annoyedly.

Ted hesitates, speaking slowly.

"Well—after the fact that I'm not sure—France," he says at last, and his mouth shuts after the word as if it never wanted to open again.

Oliver spreads both hands out hopelessly.

"Are you *never* going to get over that, you ass?"

"You didn't do the things I did," from Ted, rather difficultly. "If you had—"

"If I had I'd have been as sorry as you are, probably, that I'd knocked over the apple cart occasionally. But I wouldn't spend the rest of my life worrying about it and thinking I wasn't fit to go into decent society because of what happened to most of the A.E.F. Why you sound as if you'd committed the unpardonable sin. And it's nonsense."

"Well—thinking of Elinor—I'm not too darn sure I didn't," from Ted, dejectedly.

"That comes of being born in New England and that's all there is to it. Anyhow, it's over now, isn't it?"

"Not exactly—it comes back."

"Well, kick it every time it does."

"But you don't understand. That and—people like Elinor—" says Ted hopelessly.

"I do understand."

"You don't." And this time Ted's face has the look of a burned man.

"Well—" says Oliver, frankly puzzled. "Well, that's it. Oh, it doesn't matter. But if there was another war—"

"Oh, leave us poor people that are trying to write a couple of years before you dump us into heroes' graves by the Yang tse Kiang!"

"Another war—and bang! into the aviation." Ted muses, his face gone thin with tensity. "It could last as long as it liked for me, providing I got through before it did; you'd be living anyhow, living and somebody, and somebody who didn't give a plaintive hoot how things broke."

He sighs, and his face smooths back a little.

"Well, Lord, I've no real reason to kick, I suppose," he ends. "There are dozens of 'em like me—dozens and hundreds and thousands all over the shop. We had danger and all the physical pleasures and as much money as we wanted and the sense of command—all through the war. And then they come along and say 'it's all off, girls,' and you go back and settle down and play you've just come out of College in peace-times and maybe by the time you're forty you'll have a wife and an income if another scrap doesn't come along. And then when we find it isn't as easy to readjust as they think, they yammer around pop-eyed and say 'Oh, what wild young people—what naughty little wasters! They won't settle down and play

Puss-in-the-corner at all—and, oh dear, oh dear, how they drink and smoke and curse 'n everything!'"

"I'm awful afraid they might be right as to what's the trouble with us, though," says Oliver, didactically. "We *are* young, you know."

"Melgrove!" the conductor howls, sleepily. "Melgrove! Melgrove!"

V

The Crowe house was both small and inconveniently situated—it was twenty full minutes walk from the station and though a little box of a garage had been one of the "all modern conveniences" so fervidly painted in the real estate agent's advertisement, the Crowes had no car. It was the last house on Undercliff Road that had any pretense to sparse grass and a stubbly hedge—beyond it were sand-dunes, delusively ornamented by the signs of streets that as yet only existed in the brain of the owner of the "development," and, a quarter of a mile away, the long blue streak of the Sound.

Oliver's key clicked in the lock—this was fortunately one of the times when four-year-old Jane Ellen, who went about after sunset in a continual, piteous fear of "black men wif masks," had omitted to put the chain on the door before being carried mutinously to bed. Oliver switched on the hall light and picked up a letter and a folded note from the card tray.

> "Ted, Ollie and Dickie will share that little bijou, the sleeping porch, unless Ted prefers the third-story bathtub," the note read. "Breakfast at convenience for those that can get it themselves—otherwise at nine. And DON'T wake Dickie up.
>
> MOTHER."

Oliver passed it to Ted, who read it, grinned, and saluted, nearly knocking over the hatrack.

"For *God's* sake!" said Oliver in a piercing whisper, "Jane Ellen will think that's Indians!"

Both listened frantically for a moment, holding their breath. But there was no sound from upstairs except an occasional soft rumbling. Oliver had often wondered what would happen if the whole sleeping family chanced to breathe in and out in unison some unlucky night. He could see the papery walls blown apart like scraps of cardboard—Aunt Elsie falling, falling with her bed from her little bird-house under the eaves, giving vent to one deaf, terrified "Hey—what's that?" as she sank like Lucifer cast from Heaven inexorably down into the laundry stove, her little tight, white curls standing up on end....

Ted had removed his shoes and was making for the stairs with the exaggerated caution of a burglar in a film.

"Night!" called Oliver softly.

"G' night! Where's my bed—next the wall? Good—then I won't step on Dickie. And if you fall over me when you come in, I'll bay like a bloodhound!"

"I'll look out. Be up in a minute myself. Going to write a letter."

"So I'd already deduced, Craig Kennedy, my friend. Well, give her my love!"

He smiled like a bad little boy and disappeared round the corner. A stair creaked—they were the kind of stairs that always creaked like old women's bones, when you tried to go up them quietly. There was the sound of something soft stubbing against something hard and a muffled "*Sonofa*—"

"What's matter?"

"Oh, nothing. Blame near broke my toe on Jane Ellen's doll's porcelain head. 'S all right. 'Night."

"Night." Then in an admonitory sotto-voce, "Remember, if you wake Dickie, you've got to tell him stories till he goes to sleep again, or he'll wake up everybody else!"

"If he wakes, I'll garotte him. 'Night."

"Night."

Oliver paused for a few minutes, waiting for the crash that would proclaim that Ted had stumbled over something and waked Dickie beyond redemption. But there was nothing but a soft gurgling of water from the bathroom and then, after a while, a slight but definite addition to the distant beehive noises of sleep in the house. He smiled, moved cautiously into the dining room, sat down at the small sharp-cornered desk where all the family correspondence was carried on and from which at least one of the family a day received a grievous blow in the side while attempting to get around it; lit the shaded light above it and sat down to read his letter.

It was all Nancy, that letter, from the address, firm and straight as any promise she ever gave, but graceful as the curl of a vine-stem, gracile as her hands, with little unsuspected curlicues of humor and fancy making the stiff "t's" bend and twisting the tails of the "e's," to the little scrunched-up "Love, Nancy" at the end, as if she had squeezed it there to make it look unimportant, knowing perfectly that it was the one really important thing in the letter to him. Both would take it so and be thankful without greediness or a longing for sentimental "x's," with a sense that the thing so given must be very rich in little like a jewel, and always newly rediscovered with a shiver of pure wonder and thanking, or neither could have borne to have it written so small.

It was Nancy just as some of her clothes were Nancy, soft clear blues and first appleblossom pinks, the colors of a hardy garden that has no need for the phoenix-colors of the poppy, because it has passed the boy's necessity for talking at the top of its voice in scarlet and can hold in one shaped fastidious petal, faint-flushed with a single trembling of one serene living dye, all the colors the wise mind knows and the soul released into its ecstasy has taken for its body invisible, its body of delight most spotless, as lightning takes bright body of rapture and agony from the light clear pallor that softens a sky to night.

Oliver read the letter over twice—it was with a satisfaction like that when body and brain are fed at once, invisibly, by the same lustre of force, that he put it away. One part of it, though, left him humanly troubled enough.

"Miss Winters, the old incubus, came around and was soppy to mother as usual yesterday—the same old business—I might be studying in Paris, now, instead of teaching drawing to stupid little girls, if I hadn't 'formed' what she will call 'that unfortunate attachment.' Not that I minded, really, though I was angry enough to bite her when she gave a long undertaker's list of Penniless Authors' Brides. But it worries mother—and that worries me—and I wish she wouldn't. Forgive me, Ollie—and then that Richardson complex of mother's came up again—"

"Waiting hurts, naturally,—and I'm the person who used to wonder about girls making such a fuss about how soon they got married—but, then, Ollie, of course, I never really wanted to get married before myself and somehow that seems to make a difference. But that's the way things go—and the only thing I wish is that I was the only person to be hurt. We will, sooner or later, and it will be all the better for our not having grabbed at once—at least that's what all the old people with no emotions left are always so anxious to tell you. But they talk about it as if anybody under thirty-five who wanted to get married was acting like a three-year-old stealing jam—and that's annoying. And anyhow, it wouldn't be bad, if I weren't so silly, I suppose—"

"Waiting hurts, naturally," and that casual sentence made him chilly afraid. For to be in love, though it may force the lover to actions of impossible courage does not make him in the least courageous of himself, but only drives him by the one large fear of losing this love like a soldier pricked from behind by a bayonet over the bodies of smaller fears, or like a thief who has stolen treasure, and, hearing the cry at his heels, scales a twenty foot wall with the agile gestures of a madman. All the old-wives' and young men's club stories of everything from broken engagements to the Generic and Proven Unfaithfulness of the Female Sex brushed like dirty cobwebs for an instant across his mind. They tightened about it like silk threads—a snaky web—and for one scared instant he had a sense of being smothered in dusty feathers, whispering together and saying, "When you're a little older and a great deal wiser. When you've come to my age and know that all girls are the same. When you realize that long engagements seldom mean marriage. When—"

He put the cobwebs aside with a strain of will, for he was very tired in body, and settled himself to write to Nancy. It was not the cobwebs that hurt. The only thing that mattered was that she had been hurt on his account—was being hurt now on his account—would be hurt, and still and always on his account, not because he wanted to hurt her but because it was not within his power, but Life's, to hurt her in that respect or not.

"Oh, felicitous Nancy!" the pen began to scratch. "Your letter—"

Stupid to be so tired when he was writing to Nancy. Stupid not to find the right things to say at once when you wanted to say them so much. He dropped the pen an instant, sat back, and tried to evoke Nancy before him like a small, clear picture seen in a lens, tried to form with his will the lifeless air in front of him till it began to take on some semblance and body of her that would be better than the tired remembrances of the mind.

Often, and especially when he had thought about her intensely for a long time, the picture would not come at all or come with tantalizing incompleteness, apparently because he wanted it to be whole so much—all he could see would be a wraith of Nancy, wooden as a formal photograph, with none of her silences or mockeries about her till he felt like a painter who has somehow let the devil into his paintbox so that each stroke he makes goes a little fatally out of true from the vision in his mind till the canvas is only a crazy-quilt of reds and yellows. Now, perhaps, though, she might come, even though he was tired. He pressed the back of a hand against his eyes. She was coming to him now. He remembered one of their walks together—a walk they had taken some eight months ago, when they had been only three days engaged. Up Fifth Avenue; Forty-second Street, Forty-third, Forty-fourth, the crosstown glitter of lights, the reflected glow of Broadway, spraying the sky with dim gold-dust, begins to die a little behind them. Past pompous expensive windows full of the things that Oliver and Nancy will buy when Oliver's novel has gone into its first fifty thousand, content with the mere touch of each other's hands, they are so sure of each other now. Past people, dozens of people, getting fewer and fewer as Forty-sixth Street comes, Forty-seventh, Forty-eighth, always a little arrogantly because none of the automatic figures they pass have ever eaten friendly bread together or had fire that can burn over them like clear salt water or the knowledge that the only thing worth having in life is the hurt and gladness of that fire. Buses pass like big squares of honeycomb on wheels, crowded with pale, tired bees—the stars march slowly from the western slope to their light viewless pinnacle in the center of the heavens, walking brightly like strong men in silvered armor—the stars and the buses, the buses and the stars, either and both of as little and much account—it would not really surprise either Oliver or Nancy if the next green bus that passes should start climbing into the sky like a clumsy bird.

The first intoxication is still upon them—they have told nobody except anyone who ever sees them together—they walk tactfully and never too close, both having a horror of publicly amatory couples, but like the king's daughter—or was it Solomon's Temple?—they are all glorious within. Fifty-fifth, Fifty-sixth, Fifty-seventh—the square in front of the Plaza—that tall chopped bulky tower lit from within like a model in a toyshop window—motors purring up to its door like thin dark cats, motors purring away. The fountain with the little statue—the pool a cool dark stone cracked with the gold of the lights upon it, and near the trees of the Park, half-hidden, gold Sherman, riding, riding, Victory striding ahead of him with a golden palm.

Ahead of them too goes Victory, over fear, over doubt, over littleness, her gold shoes ring like the noise of a sparkling sword, her steps are swift. They stand for an instant, hands locked, looking back at the long roller-coaster swoop of the Avenue, listening to the roll of tired wheels, the faint horns, the loud horns. They know each other now—their hands grip tighter—in the wandering instant the whole background of streets and tall buildings passes like breath from a mirror—for the instant without breath or clamor, they exist together, one being, and the being has neither flesh to use the senses too clumsily, nor human thoughts to rust at the will, but lives with the strength of a thunder and the heedlessness of a wave in a wide and bright eternity of the unspoken.

"All the same," says Nancy, when the moment passes, lifting a shoe with the concern of a kitten that has just discovered a thorn in its paw, "New York pavements are certainly *hard* on loving feet."

VI

So the picture came. And other pictures like it. And since the living that had made them was past for a little they were both fainter and in a measure brighter with more elfin colors than even that living had been which had made them glow at first. White memory had taken them into her long house of silence where everything is cool with the silver of Spring rain on leaves, she had washed from them the human pettiness, the human separateness, the human insufficiency to express the best that must come in any mortal relationship that lasts longer than the hour. They were not better in memory than they had been when lived, for the best remembrance makes only brilliant ghosts, but they were in their dim measure nearer the soul's perfection, for the tricks of the sounding board of the mind and the feckless instrument of the body had been put away. "We've had infinites already—infinites," thought Oliver, and didn't care about the ludicrous ineptness of the words. He smiled, turning back to the unwritten letter. If they hadn't had infinites already—he supposed they wouldn't want more so badly right now. He smiled, but this time without humor. It had all seemed so easy at first.

Nancy had been in Paris at fourteen before "business reverses" of the kind that mild, capable-looking men like Mr. Ellicott seem to attract, as a gingerbread man draws wasps, when they are about fifty, had reduced him to a position as chief bookkeeper and taken Nancy out of her first year in Farmington. Oliver had spent nine months on a graduate scholarship in Paris and Provence in 1919. Both had friends there and argued long playful hours planning just what sort of a magnificently cheap apartment on the *Rive Gauche* they would have when they went back.

For they were going back—they had been brilliantly sure of it—Oliver had only to finish his novel that was so much better already than any novel Nancy had ever read—sell a number of copies of it that seemed absurdly small in proportion to the population of America—and then they could live where they pleased and Oliver could compose Great Works and Nancy get ahead with her very real and delicate talent for etching instead of having to do fashion-drawings of slinky simperers in Lucile dresses or appetite-arousing paintings of great cans of tomato soup. But that had been eight months ago. Vanamee and Company's—the neat vice-president talking to Oliver—"a young hustler has every chance in the world of getting ahead here, Mr. Crowe. You speak French? Well, we have been thinking for some time of establishing branch-offices in Europe." The chance of a stop-gap job in St. Louis for Nancy, where she could be with her family for a while—she really ought to be with them a couple of months at least, if she and Oliver were to be married so soon. The hopeful parting in the Grand Central—"But, Nancy, you're sure you wouldn't mind going across second-class?"

"Why Ollie, dear, how silly! Why, what would it matter?" "All right, then, and remember, I'll wire *just* as soon as things really start to break—"

And then for eight months, nothing at all but letters and letters, except two times, once in New York, once in St. Louis, when both had spent painful savings because they simply had to see each other again, since even the best letters were only doll-house food you could look at and wish you could eat— and both had tried so hard to make each disappearing minute perfect before they had to catch trains again that the effort left them tired as jugglers who have been balancing too many plates and edgy at each other for no cause in the world except the unfairness that they could only have each other now for so short a time. And the people, the vast unescapable horde of the dull-but-nice or the merely dull who saw in their meetings nothing either particularly spectacular or pitiful or worth applause.

And always after the parting, a little crippled doubt tapping its crutches along the alleys of either mind. "Do I *really?* Because if I do, how can I be so tired sometimes with her, with him? And why can't I say more and do more and be more when he, when she? And everybody says. And they're older than we are—mightn't it be true? And—" And then, remorsefully, the next day, all doubt burnt out by the clear hurt of absence. "Oh how could I! When it is real—when it is like that—when it is the only thing worth while in the world!"

But absence and meetings of this sort told on them inescapably, and both being, unfortunately, of a rather high-strung intelligence and youth, recognized it, no matter how much consciousness might deny it, and wondered sometimes, rather pitiably, why they couldn't be always at one temperature, like lovers in poetry, and why either should ever worry or hurt the other when they loved. Any middle-aged person could and did tell them that they were now really learning something about love—omitting the small fact that Pain, though he comes with the highest literary recommendations is really not the wisest teacher of all in such matters—all of which helped the constant nervous and psychological strain on both as little as a Latin exorcism would help a fever. For the very reason that they wished to be true in their love, they said things in their letters that a spoken word or a gesture would have explained in an instant but that no printed alphabet could; and so they often hurt each other while meaning and trying to help all they could.

Not quite as easy as it had seemed at first—oh, not on your life not, thought Oliver, rousing out of a gloomy muse. And then there was the writing he wanted to do—and Nancy's etching—"our damn careers" they had called them—but those *were* the things they did best—and neither had had even tolerable working conditions recently—

Well, sufficient to the day was the evil thereof—that was one of those safe Bible-texts you seemed to find more and more use for the older you grew. Bible-texts. It was lucky tomorrow was Sunday when slaves of the alarm-clock had peace. Oliver straightened his shoulders unconsciously and turned back to the blank paper. He did love Nancy. He did love Nancy. That was all that counted.

> "Oh, felicitous Nancy!
> Your letter was—"

VII

The water was a broken glass of blue, sunstruck waves—there were few swimmers in it where the two friends went in next morning, for the beach proper with its bath-houses and float was nearly a quarter of a mile down. Oliver could see Margaret's red cap bobbing twenty yards out as he tried the water cautiously with curling toes, and, much farther out, a blue cap and the flash of an arm going suddenly under. Mrs. Severance, the friend Louise had brought out for the week-end, he supposed; she swam remarkably for a woman. He swam well enough himself and couldn't give her two yards in the hundred. Ted stood beside him, both tingling a little at the fresh of the salt air. "Wow!" and they plunged.

A mock race followed for twenty yards—then Oliver curved off to duck Margaret, already screaming and paddling at his approach, while Ted kept on.

He swam face deep, catching short breaths under the crook of his arm, burying himself in the live blue running sparkle, every muscle stretched as if he were trying to rub all the staleness that can come to the mind and the restless pricklings that will always worry the body clean from him, like a snake's cast skin, against the wet rough hands of the water. There—it was working—the flesh was compact and separate no longer—he felt it dissolve into the salt push of spray—become one with that long blue body of wave that stretched fluently radiant for miles and miles till it too was no more identity but only sea, receiving the sun, without thought, without limbs, without

Stephen Vincent Benet

pain. He sprinted with the last breath he had in him to annihilation in that light lustrous firmament. Then his flung-out hand struck something firm and smooth. With the momentary twinge of a jarred toe, he stopped in the middle of a stroke, grabbed at the firm thing unthinkingly, felt it slip away from him, trod water and came up gasping.

"Oh, I'm *horribly* sorry!" Gurgle and choke at water gone the wrong way. "Honestly—what a dumb-bell trick! but I didn't see you at *all* and with the whole Sound to swim in I thought I was safe—"

He rubbed the water out of his eyes. A woman in a blue cap. Pretty, too—not one of the pretty kind that look like drenched paper-dolls in swimming.

"Don't apologize—it's all my fault, really. I should have heard you coming, I suppose, but I was floating and my ears were under water—and this cap! You did scare me a little, though; I didn't know there was anyone else in miles—"

She smiled frankly. Ted got another look at her and decided that pretty was hardly right. Beautiful, perhaps, but you couldn't tell with her hair that way under her cap.

"You're Mr. Billett, aren't you? Louise said last night that her brother was bringing a friend over Sunday. She also said that she'd introduce us—but we seem to have done that."

"Rather. Introduction by drowning. The latest cleverness in Newport circles—see 'Mode.' And you're Mrs. Severance."

"Yes. Nice water."

"Perfect."

A third look—a fairly long one—left Ted still puzzled. Age—thirty? thirty-five? Swims perfectly. On "Mode." Wide eyes, sea-blue, sea-changing. An odd nose that succeeded in being beautiful in spite of itself. A rather full small mouth, not loose with sense nor rigid with things controlled, but a mouth that would suck like a bee at the last and tiniest drop of any physical sweet which the chin and the eyes had once decided to want. The eyes measure, the mouth asks, the cleft chin finds the way. A face neither content, nor easily to be contented—in repose it is neither happy nor unhappy but only matured. Louise's friend—that was funny—Louise had such an ideal simplicity of mind. Well—

"If you float—after a while you don't know quite where you're floating," said Mrs. Severance's voice detachedly.

Ted made no answer but turned over, spreading out his arms. For a few moments they lay like corpses on the blue swelling round of the water looking straight through infinite distance into the thin faint vapor of the sky.

"Yes, I see what you mean."

"We might be clouds, almost, mightn't we?" with a slow following note of laughter.

Ted looked deeper into the sky, half-closing his eyelids. It seemed to take his body from him completely, to leave him nothing but a naked soothed consciousness, rising and falling, a petal on a swinging bough, in the heart of blue quietude like the quiet of an open place in a forest empty with evening.

"Clouds," said Mrs. Severance's voice, turning the word to a sound breathed lightly through the curled and husky gold of a forest-horn.

Through the midst of his sea-drowsiness a queer thought came to Ted. This had happened before, in sleep perhaps, in a book he had read—Oliver's novel, possibly, he thought and smiled. Lying alone on a roof of blue water, and yet not lying alone, for there was that slow warm voice that talked from time to time and came into the mind on tiptoe like the creeping of

Stephen Vincent Benet

soft-shoed, hasteless, fire. You stretched your hands to the fire and let it warm you and soon your whole body was warm and pleased and alive. That was when you were alive past measure, when all of you had been made warm as a cat fed after being hungry, and the cat arose from its warmth and went walking on velvet paws, stretching sleek legs, sleek body, slowly and exquisitely under the firelight, heavy with warmth, but ready at the instant signal of the small burning thing in its mind to turn like a black butterfly and dance a slow seeking dance with the shadows of the fire that flickered like leaves in light wind, desirable, impalpable and wavering, never to be quite torn down from the wall and eaten and so possessed. But there was an odd thirsty satisfaction in trying to tear the shadows.

Fantastic. He had not been so fantastic for a long time.

"And tomorrow there's 'Mode.' And fashion-plates. *And* Greenwich Villagers," said the voice of Mrs. Severance. He made some reply impatiently, disliking the sound of his own voice—hers fitted with the dream. When had he been this before?

The Morte d'Arthur—the two with a sword between.

He sank deeper, deeper, into the glow of that imagined firelight—the flame was cooler than water to walk through—that time he had almost taken a turning shadow into his hand. The sword between—only here there was no sword. If he reached out his hand he knew just how the hand that he touched would feel, cool and firm, like that flame. Cool and silent.

There must have been something, somewhere, to make him remember....

He remembered.

A minute later Oliver had splashed up to them, shouting "A rescue! A rescue! Guests Drown While Host Looks On

Smilingly! What's the matter, Ted, you look as if you wanted to turn into a submarine? Got cramp?"

Stephen Vincent Benet

VIII

Mrs. Crowe relaxed a little for the first tired minute of her day. Sunday dinner was nearly over, and though, in one way, the best meal in the week for her because all her children were sure to be at home, it was apt to be pure purgatory on a hot day, with Sheba dawdling and grumbling and Rosalind spilling pea-soup on her Sunday dress, and Aunt Elsie's deafness increased by the weather to the point of mild imbecility.

She had been a little afraid today, especially with two guests and the grandchildren rampant after church, and the extra leaf in the table that squeezed Colonel Crowe almost into the sideboard and herself nearly out of the window and made the serving of a meal a series of passings of over-hot plates from hand to hand, exposed to the piracies of Jane Ellen. But it had gone off better than she could have hoped. Colonel Crowe had not absent-mindedly begun to serve vegetables with a teaspoon, Aunt Elsie had not dissolved in tears and tottered away from the table at some imagined rudeness of Dickie's, and Jane Ellen had not once had a chance to take off her drawers.

"Ice tea!" said the avid voice of Jane Ellen in her ear. "Ice tea!"

Mrs. Crowe filled the glass and submitted a request for "please" mechanically. She wondered, rather idly, if she would spend her time in purgatory serving millions of Jane Ellens with iced tea.

"Ahem!" That was Colonel Crowe. "But you should have known us in the days of our greatness, Mrs. Severance. When I was king of Estancia—"

"I'd rather have you like this, Colonel Crowe, really. I've always wanted big families and never had one to live in—"

"Heard from Nancy recently, Oliver?" from Margaret, slightly satiric.

"Why yes, Margie, now and then. Not as often as you've heard from Stu Winthrop probably but—"

"Motha, can I have some suga on my booberrish? Motha, can I have some suga on my booberrish? Motha—*peesh*!"

"Oh, hush a minute, Rosalind dear. I don't know, Oliver. I'll speak to Mr. Field about it if you like. I should think they'd take little sketches like a couple of those Nancy showed you—though they aren't quite smart-alecky enough for 'Mode'—"
"Grandfather, Grandfather! How old would you be if you were as old as Methusaleh? Are you older than he is? *Grandfather!*"

Entrance and exit of a worried Sheba with the empty dish of blueberries, marred only by Jane Ellen's sudden cries of "Stop thief!"

Mrs. Crowe tried to think a little ahead. Tomorrow. Ice. Butter. Laundry. Oliver's breakfast early again. Louise—poor Louise—two years and a half since Clifford Lychgate died. How curious life was; how curious and careless and inconsecutive. The thought of how much she hoped Oliver's novel would succeed and the question as to whether the Thebes grocer who delivered by motor-truck would be cheaper than the similar Melgrove bandit in the long run mixed uneasily in her mind.

Rosalind had seemed droopy that morning—more green crab-apples probably. Aunt Elsie's gout. Oliver's marriage—she had been so relieved about Nancy ever since she had met her, though it had been hard to reconcile domestic virtues with Nancy's bobbed hair. She would make Oliver happy, though, and that was the main thing. She was really sweet—a sweet girl. Long engagements. Too bad, too bad. Something *must* be done about the stair carpet, the children were tearing it to pieces. "Ice tea! Ice tea!"

"No, Jane Ellen."

"Yash."

"No, darling."

"Peesh yash?"

"No. Now be a good little girl and run out and play quietly, not right in the middle of the broiling sun."

"And so Lizzie said, 'Very well, but if I do take that medicine my death will be wholly on your responsibility!'" with a sense of climax.

"But I really would like to, Mrs. Severance, if you can ever spare the time."

Ted and Louise's friend seemed to be getting along very well. That was nice—so often Oliver's friends and Louise's didn't. It seemed odd that Mrs. Severance should be working on "Mode"—surely a girl of her obvious looks and intelligence left with no children to support—some nice man—A lady, too, by her voice, though there was a trifle of something—

She only hoped Mrs. Severance didn't think them all too crowded and noisy. It was a little hard on the three children to have such an—intimate—home when they brought friends.

"I think we'd better have coffee out on the porch, don't you?" That meant argument with Sheba later but an hour's cool and talk without having to shout across the dear little children was worth the argument.

Everybody got up, Ted being rather gallant to Mrs. Severance. Oliver looked worried today, worried and tired. She hoped it wasn't about Nancy and the engagement. What a miserable thing money was to make so much difference.

"Mrs. Severance—"

"Mr. Billett—"

Louise's friend was certainly attractive. That wonderful red-gold hair—"setter color" her sister had always called it of her own. She must write her sister. Mrs. Severance—an odd name. She rather wished, though, that her face wouldn't turn faintly hard like that sometimes.

"No, Dickie. No chocolate unless your mother says you can have it. No, Rosalind, if mother says not, you *certainly* cannot go over and play at the Rogers',—they have a paralytic grandmother who is very nervous."

Well, that was over. And now, for a few brief instants there would be quiet and a chance to relax and really see something of Oliver. Mrs. Crowe started moving slowly towards the door. Ted and Mrs. Severance blocked the way, talking rather intimately, she thought, for people who had only known each other a few hours; but then that was the modern way. Then Ted saw her and seemed to wake up with a jump from whatever mild dream possessed him, and Mrs. Severance turned toward her.

"It's so *comfortable* being out here, always," she said very naturally and kindly, but Mrs. Crowe did not reply at once to the pretty speech. Instead she flushed deeply and bent over something small and white on the chair with the dictionary in it that had been next to hers. Jane Ellen had finally succeeded in taking off her drawers.

IX

Ted and Oliver were down at the beach at Southampton two Sundays later—week-end guests of Peter Piper—the three had been classmates at Yale and the friendship had not lapsed like so many because Peter happened to be rich and Ted and Oliver poor. And then there was always Elinor, Peter's sister— Ted seemed, to Oliver's amused vision, at least, to be looking at Elinor with the hungry eyes of a man seeing a delicate, longed-for dream made flesh just at present instead of a girl he had known since she first put up her hair. How nice that would be if it happened, thought Oliver, match-makingly— how very nice indeed! Best thing in the world for Ted—and Elinor too—if Ted would only get away from his curiously Puritan idea that a few minor lapses from New England morality in France constituted the unpardonable sin, at least as far as marrying a nice girl was concerned. He stretched back lazily, digging elbows into the warm sand.

The day had really been too hot for anything more vigorous than "just lying around in the sun like those funny kinds of lizards," as Peter put it, and besides, he and Oliver had an offensive-defensive alliance of The Country's Tiredest Young Business Men and insisted that their only function in life was to be gently and graciously amused. And certainly the spectacle about them was one to provide amusement in the extreme for even the most mildly satiric mind.

It was the beach's most crowded hour and the short strip of sand in front of the most fashionable and uncomfortable place to bathe on Long Island was gay as a patch of exhibition sweet-peas with every shade of vivid or delicate color. It was a triumph of women—the whole glittering, moving bouquet of stripes and patterns and tints that wandered slowly from one striped parasol-mushroom to the next—the men, in their bathing suits or white flannels seemed as unimportant if necessary furniture as slaves in an Eastern court. The women dominated, from the jingle of the bags in the hands of the dowagers and the faint, protesting creak of their corsets as they picked their way as delicately as fat, gorgeous macaws across the sand, to the sound of their daughters' voices, musical as a pigeon-loft, as they chattered catchwords at each other and their partners, or occasionally, very occasionally, dipped in for a three-minute swim. Moreover, and supremely, it was a triumph of ritual, and such ritual as reminded Oliver a little of the curious, unanimous and apparently meaningless movements of a colony of penguins, for the entire assemblage had arrived around, twelve o'clock and by a quarter past one not one of them would be left. That was law as unwritten and unbreakable as that law which governs the migratory habits of wild geese. And within that little more than an hour possibly one-third of them would go as far as wetting their hands in the water—all the rest had come for the single reason of seeing and being seen. It was all extremely American and, on the whole, rather superb, Oliver thought as he and Peter moved over nearer to the parasol that sheltered Elinor and Ted.

"I wish it was Egypt," said Peter languidly. "Any more peppermints left, El? No—well, Ted never could restrain himself when it came to food. I wish it was Egypt," he repeated, making Elinor's left foot a pillow for his head.

"Well, it's hot enough," from Oliver, dozingly. "Ah—oo—it's *hot*!"

"I know, but just think," Peter chuckled. "Clothes," he explained cryptically, "Mrs. Willamette in a Cleopatra nightie—what sport! And besides, I should make a magnificent Egyptian. Magnificent." He yawned immensely. "In the first place, of course, I should paint myself a brilliant orange—"

The Egyptians. An odd wonder rose in Ted—a wonder as to whether one of those stripped and hook-nosed slaves of the bondage before Moses had ever happened to stand up for a moment to wipe the sweat out of his eyes before he bent again to his task of making bricks without straw and seen a princess of the Egyptians carried along past the quarries.

"Tell us a story, El," from Oliver in the voice of one who is sleep-walking. "A nice quiet story—the Three Bears or Giant the Jack Killer—oh heaven, I *must* be asleep—but you know, anything like that—"

"You really want a story?" Elinor's voice was reticently mocking. "A story for good little boys?"

"Oh, *yes!*" from Peter, his clasped hands stretched toward her in an attitude of absurd supplication. "All in nice little words of one syllable or we won't understand."

"Well, once there were three little girls named Elsie, Lacie and Tillie and they lived in the bottom of a well."

"What *kind* of a well?" Oliver had caught the cue at once.

"A treacle well—"

* * * * *

She went on with the Dormouse's Tale, but Ted, for once, hardly heard her—his mind was too busy with its odd, Egyptological dream.

The princess who looked like Elinor. Her slaves would come first—a fat bawling eunuch, all one black glisten like new patent-leather, striking with a silver rod to clear dogs and crocodiles and Israelites out of the way. Then the litter—and a flash between curtains blown aside for an instant—and Hook

Nose gazing and gazing—all the fine fighting curses of David on the infidel, that he had muttered sourly under breath all day, blowing away from him like sand from the face of a sphinx.

Pomp sounding in brass and cries all around the litter like the boasting color of a trumpet—but in the litter not pomp but fineness passing. Fineness of youth untouched, from the clear contrast of white skin and crow-black hair to the hands that had the little stirrings of moon-moths against the green robe. Fineness of mind that will not admit the unescapable minor dirts of living, however much it may see them, a mind temperate with reticence and gentleness, seeing not life itself but its own delighted dream of it, a heart that had had few shocks as yet, and never the ones that the heart must be mailed or masked to withstand. The thing that passed had been continually sheltered, exquisitely guarded from the stronger airs of life as priests might guard a lotus, and yet it was neither tenderly unhealthy nor sumptuously weak. A lotus—that was it—and Hook Nose stood looking at the lotus—and because it was innocent he filled his eyes with it. And then it passed and its music went out of the mind.

"*Ted*!"

"What? What? Oh, yeah—sorry, Elinor, I wasn't paying proper attention."

"You mean you were asleep, you big cheese!" from Peter.

"I wasn't—just thinking," and seeing that this only brought raucous mirth from both Peter and Oliver, "Oh, shut up, you apes! Were you asking me something, El?"

It was rather a change to come back from Elinor in scarab robes being carried along in a litter to Elinor sitting beside him in a bathing suit. But hardly an unpleasant change.

"I've forgotten how it goes on—the Dormouse—after 'Well

in.' Do you remember?"

"Nope. Look it up when we get back. And anyhow—"
"What?"

"Game called for to-day. The Lirrups have started looking important—that means it's about ten minutes of, they always leave on the dot. Well—" and Peter rose, scattering sand. "We must obey our social calendar, my prominent young friends— just think how awful it would be if we were the last to go. Race you half-way to the float and back, Ted."

"You're on," and the next few minutes were splashingly athletic.

Going back to the bath-house, though, Ted laughed at himself rather whimsically. That extraordinary day-dream of the slave and the Elinor Princess! It helped sometimes, to make pictures of the very impossible—even of things as impossible as that. If Elinor had only been older before the war came along and changed so much.

He saw another little mental photograph, the kind of photograph, he mused, that sleekly shabby Frenchmen slip from under views of the Vendome Column and Napoleon's Tomb when they are trying to sell tourists picture post-cards outside the Cafe de la Paix. Judged by American standards the work would be called rather frank. It was all interior—the interior of a room in a Montmartre hotel—and there were two people in it to help out the composition—and the face of one seemed somehow to be rather deathly familiar—

That, and Elinor. Why, Hook Nose could "reform" all the rest of his life in accordance with the highest dictionary standards—and still he wouldn't be fit to look at his princess, even from inside a cage.

Also, if you happened to be of a certain analytic temperament you could see what was happening to yourself all the while quite plainly—oh, much too plainly!—and yet that seemed to make very little difference in its going on happening. There was Mrs. Severance, for instance. He had been seeing quite a good deal of Mrs. Severance lately.

"Oh, Ted!" from Peter next door. "Snap it up, old keed, or we'll all of us be late for lunch."

They had just sat down to lunch and Peter was complaining that the whipped cream on the soup made him feel as if he were eating cotton-batting, when a servant materialized noiselessly beside Oliver's chair.

"Telephone for you, Mr. Crowe. Western Union calling."

Oliver jumped up with suspicious alacrity. "Oh, love, love, love!" crooned Peter. "Oh, love, love, love!" Oliver flushed. "Don't swipe all my butter, you simple cynic!" He knew what it was, of course.

"This is Oliver Crowe talking. Will you give me the telegram?"

Nancy and Oliver, finding Sunday mails of a dilatory unsatisfactoriness, had made a compact to use the wire on that day instead. And even now Oliver never listened to the mechanical buzz of Central's voice in his ear without a little pulse of the heart. It seemed to bring Nancy nearer than letters could, somehow. Nancy had an imperial contempt for boiling down attractive sentences to the necessary ten or twenty words. This time, though, the telegram was short.

"Mr. Oliver Crowe, care Peter Piper, Southampton," clicked Central dispassionately. "I hate St. Louis. I would give anything in the world if we could only see each other for twenty-four hours. Love. Signed, Nancy."

And Oliver, after hanging up the receiver, went back to the dining-room with worry barking and running around his mind like a spoiled puppy, wondering savagely why so many rocking-chair people took a *crepey* pleasure in saying it was good for young people in love to have to wait.

X

Tea for two at the Gondolier, that newest and quotation-marked "Quaintest" of Village tea rooms. The chief points in the Gondolier's "quaintness" seem to be that it is chopped up into as many little partitions as a roulette wheel and that all food has to be carried up from a cellar that imparts even to orange marmalade a faint persuasive odor of somebody else's wash. Still, during the last eight months, the Gondolier has been a radical bookstore devoted to bloody red pamphlets, a batik shop full of strange limp garments ornamented with decorative squiggles, and a Roumanian Restaurant called "The Brodska" whose menu seemed to consist almost entirely of old fish and maraschino cherries.

The wispy little woman from Des Moines who conducts the Gondolier at present in a series of timid continual flutters at actually leading the life of the Bohemian untamed, and who gives all the young hungry-looking men extra slices of toast because any one of them might be Vachel Lindsay in disguise, will fail in another six weeks and then the Gondolier may turn into anything from a Free Verse Tavern to a Meeting Hall for the Friends of Slovak Freedom. But at present, the tea is much too good for the price in spite of its inescapable laundry tang, and there is a flat green bowl full of Japanese iris bulbs in the window—the second of which pleases Mrs. Severance and the first Ted.

Besides like most establishments on the verge of bankruptcy, it is such a quiet place to talk—the only other two people in it are a boy with startled hair and an orange smock and a cigaretty girl called Tommy, and she is far too busy telling him that that dream about wearing a necklace of flying-fish shows a dangerous inferiority complex even to comment caustically on strangers from uptown who *will* intrude on the dear Village.

"Funny stuff—dreams," says Ted uneasily, catching at overheard phrases for a conversational jumping-off place. His mind, always a little on edge now with work and bad feeding, has been too busy since they came in comparing Rose Severance with Elinor Piper, and wondering why, when one is so like a golden-skinned August pear and the other a branch of winter blackberries against snow just fallen, it is not as good but somehow warmer to think of the first against your touch than the second, to leave him wholly at ease.

"Yes—funny stuff," Mrs. Severance's voice is musically quiet. "And then you tell them to people who pretend to know all about what they mean—and then—" She shrugs shoulders at the Freudian two across the shoulder-high partition.

"But you don't believe in all this psycho-analysis tosh, do you?"

She hesitates. "A little, yes. Like the old woman and ghosts. I may not believe in it but I'm afraid of it, rather."

She gives him a steady look—her eyes go deep. It is not so much the intensity of the look as its haltingness that makes warmth go over him.

"Shall we tell our dreams—the favorite ones, I mean? Play fair if we do, remember," she adds slowly.

"Not if you're really afraid."

"I? But it's just because I am afraid that I really should, you know. Like going into a dark room when you don't want to."

"But they can't be as scary as *that*, surely." Ted's voice is a little false. Both are watching each other intently now—he with a puzzled sense of lazy enveloping firelight.

"Well, shall I begin? After all this *is* tea in the Village."

"I should be very much interested indeed, Mrs. Severance," says Ted rather gravely. "Check!" "How official you sound—almost as if you had a lot of those funny little machines all the modern doctors use and were going to mail me off to your pet sanatorium at once because you'd asked me what green reminded me of and I said 'cheese' instead of 'trees.' And anyhow, I never have any startling dreams—only silly ones—much too silly to tell—"

"Please go on." Ted's voice has really become quite clinical.

"Oh very well. They don't count when you only have them once—just when they keep coming back and back to you—isn't that it?"

"I believe so."

Mrs. Severance's eyes waver a little—her mouth seeking for the proper kind of dream.

"It's not much but it comes quite regularly—the most punctual, old-fashioned-servant sort of a dream.

"It doesn't begin with sleep, you know—it begins with waking. At least it's just as if I were in my own bed in my own apartment and then gradually I started to wake. You know how you can feel that somebody else is in the room though you can't see them—that's the feeling. And, of course being a normal American business woman, my first idea is—burglars. And I'm very cowardly for a minute. Then the cowardice passes and I decide to get up and see what it is.

"It *is* somebody else—or something—but nobody I think that

I ever really knew. And at first I don't want to walk toward it—and then I do because it keeps pulling me in spite of myself. So I go to it—hands out so I won't knock over things.

"And then I touch it—or him—or her—and I'm suddenly very, very happy.

"That's all.

"And now, Dr. Billett, what would you say of my case?"

Ted's eyes are glowing—in the middle of her description his heart has begun to knock to a hidden pulse, insistent and soft as the drum of gloved fingers on velvet. He picks words carefully.

"I should say—Mrs. Severance—that there was something you needed and wanted and didn't have at present. And that you would probably have it—in the end."

She laughs a little. "Rather cryptic, isn't that, doctor? And you'd prescribe?"

"Prescribe? 'It's an awkward matter to play with souls.'"

"And trouble enough to save your own," she completes the quotation. "Yes, that's true enough—though I'm sorry you can't even tell me to use this twice a day in half a glass of water and that other directly after each meal. I think I'll have to be a little more definite when it comes to your turn—if it does come."

"Oh it will." But instead of beginning, he raises his eyes to her again. This time there is a heaviness like sleep on both, a heaviness that draws both together inaudibly and down, and down, as if they were sinking through piled thickness on thickness of warm, sweet-scented grass. Odd faces come into both minds and vanish as if flickered off a film—to Rose Severance, a man narrow and flat as if he were cut out of thin grey paper, talking, talking in a voice as dry and rattling as a flapping windowblind of their "vacation" together and a house with a little garden where she can sew and he can putter around,—to Ted, Elinor Piper, the profile pure as if it were painted on water, passing like water flowing from the earth in springs, in its haughty temperance, its retired beauty, its murmurous quiet—other faces, some trembling as if touched with light flames, some calm, some merely grotesque with longing or too much pleasure—all these pass. A great nearness, fiercer and more slumbrous than any nearness of body takes their place. It wraps the two closer and closer, a spider spinning a soft web out of petals, folding the two with swathes and swathes of its heavy, fragrant silk.

"Oh—mine—isn't anything," says Ted rather unsteadily, after the moment. "Only looking at firelight and wanting to take the coals in my hands."

Rose's voice is firmer than his but her mouth is still moved with content at the thing it has desired being brought nearer.

"I really can't prescribe on as little evidence as that," she says with music come back to her voice in the strength of a running wave. "I can only repeat what you told me. That there was something you needed—and wanted"—she is mocking now—"and didn't have at present. And that you would probably— what was it?—oh yes—have it, in the end."

The wispy little woman has crept up to Ted's elbow with an illegible bill. Rose has spoken slowly to give her time to get there—it is always so much better to choose your own most effective background for really affecting scenes.

"And now I really must be getting back," she cuts in briskly, her fingers playing with a hat that certainly needs no rearrangement, when Ted, after absent-mindedly paying the bill, is starting to speak in the voice of one still sleep-walking.

"But it *was* delightful, Mr. Billett—I love talking about myself

Stephen Vincent Benet

and you were really very sweet to listen so nicely." She has definitely risen. Ted must, too. "We must do it again some time soon—I'm going to see if there aren't any of those books with long German names drifting around 'Mode' somewhere so that I'll be able to simply stun you with my erudition the next time we talk over dreams."

They are at the door now, she guiding him toward it as imperceptibly and skillfully as if she controlled him by wireless.

"And it isn't fair of me to let you give all the parties—it simply isn't. Couldn't you come up to dinner in my little apartment sometime—it really isn't unconventional, especially for anyone who's once seen my pattern of an English maid—"

Sunlight and Minetta Lane again—and whatever Ted may want to say out of his walking trance—this is certainly no place where any of it can be said.

XI

Oliver Crowe, at his desk in the copy-department of Vanamee and Co.'s, has been spending most of the afternoon twiddling pencils and reading and rereading two letters out of his pocket instead of righteously thinking up layouts for the new United Steel Frame Pulley Campaign. He realizes that the layouts are important—that has been brought to his attention already by several pink memoranda from Mr. Delier, the head of the department—but an immense distaste for all things in general and advertising in particular has overwhelmed him all day. He looks around the big, brightly lighted room with a stupefied sort of loathing—advertising does not suit him—he is doing all he can at it because of Nancy—but he simply does not seem to get the hang of the thing even after eight months odd and he is conscious of the fact that the Powers that be are already looking at him with distrustful eyes, in spite of his occasional flashes of brilliance. If he could only get *out* of it—get into something where his particular kind of mind and training would be useful—oh well—he grunts and turns back to his private affairs.

The letter from Easten of Columbiac Magazines—kindly enough—but all hope of selling the serial rights of his novel gone glimmering because of it—Easten was the last chance, the last and the best. "If you could see your way to making short stories out of the incidents I have named, I should be very much interested—" but even so, two short stories won't bring in enough to marry on, even if he can do them to Easten's satisfaction—and the novel couldn't come out as a book now till late spring—and Oliver has too many friends who dabble in writing to have any more confidence in book royalties than he would have in systems for beating the bank at roulette. Well, *that's* over—and a year's work with it—and all the dreams he and Nancy had of getting married at once.

Those pulley layouts have to be fixed up sometime. What can you say about a pulley—what *can* you say? "The United Steel Frame Pulley—Oh Man, There's a Hog for Work!" Oliver turns the cheap phrase in his mind, hating its shoddiness, hating the fact that such shoddiness is the only stuff with which he can deal.

Sanely considered, he supposes he hasn't any business using up a month's meagre savings and three small checks for poems that he has hoarded since April in going out to St. Louis Friday. Mr. Alley wasn't too pleased with letting him take Saturday and half Monday off to do it, too. But then there was that telegram ten days ago. "I'd give anything in the world if we could only see each other—" and after other letters unsatisfactorily brief, the letter that came Monday "I have such grand news, Ollie dear, at least it may be grand if it works out—but oh, dear, I do want to see you about it without tangling it up in letters that don't really explain. Can't you make it—even a few hours would be long enough to talk it all over—and I do so want to see you and really talk! Please wire me, if you can."

Grand news—what kind he wondered—and dully thought that he couldn't see her, of course, and then suddenly knew that he must. After all, there didn't seem to be much use in saving for the sake of saving when all the saving you could possibly do didn't bring you one real inch nearer to what you really wanted. *Apres moi le deluge—apres ca le deluge*—it might even come to that this time, they were both so tired—and he viewed the prospect as a man mortally hurt might view the gradual failing of sun and sky above him, with hopelessness complete as a cloud in that sky, but with heart and brain too beaten now to be surprised with either agony or fear. They must see each other—they were neither of them quiet people who could love forever at a distance without real hope. Great Lord, if he and Nancy could ever have one definite basis to work on, one definite hope of money in the future no matter how far off that was—But the present uncertainty—They couldn't keep on like this—no two people in the world could be expected to keep on.

Nancy. He is seeing Nancy, the way she half-lifts her head when she has been teasing and suddenly becomes remorseful and wants him to know how much she does love him instead.

XII

A hot night in the Pullman——too hot to sleep in anything but a series of uneasy drowsings and wakings. Smell of blankets and cinders and general unwashedness—noise of clacketing wheels and a hysterical whistle—anyhow each sweaty hour brings St. Louis and Nancy nearer. St. *Nancy*, St. *Nancy*, St. *Nancy*, says the sleepless racket of the wheels, but the peevish electric fan at the end of the corridor keeps buzzing to itself like a fly caught in a trap. "And then I got married you see—and then I got married you see—and when you get married you aren't a free lance—you aren't a free lance—you're *settled!*"

It will have to be pretty grand news indeed that Nancy has to make up for this last week and the buzz of the electric fan, thinks Oliver, twisting from one side of his stuffy berth to the other like an uneasy sardine.

XIII

"More beans, Oliver," says Mrs. Ellicott in a voice like thin syrup, her "generous" voice. The generous voice is used whenever Mrs. Ellicott wants to show herself a person of incredibly scrupulous fairness before that bodiless assemblage of old women in black that constitute the They who Say—and so it is used to Oliver nearly all the time.

"No thank you, Mrs. Ellicott." Oliver manages to look at her politely enough as he speaks but then his eyes go straight back to Nancy and stay there as if they wished to be considered permanent attachments. All Oliver has been able to realize for the last two hours is the mere declarative fact that she is *there*.

"Nancy!"

"No, thanks, mother."

And Nancy in her turn looks once swiftly at her mother, sitting there at the end of the table like a faded grey sparrow whose feathers make it uncomfortable. It isn't feathers, though, really—its only Oliver. Why can't mother get reconciled to Oliver—why *can't* she—and if she can't, why doesn't she come out and say so instead of trying to be generous to Oliver when she doesn't want to while he's there and then saying mean things when he's away because she can't help it?

"Stanley?"

Stephen Vincent Benet

"Why, no, my dear—no—yes, a few, perhaps—I might reconsider—only a few, my dear,"—his voice does not do anything as definite as cease—it merely becomes ineffectual as Mrs. Ellicott heaps his plate. He then looks at the beans as if he hadn't the slightest idea where they came from but supposes as long as they are there they must be got away with somehow, and starts putting them into his mouth as mechanically as if they were pennies and he a slot-machine.

It is hot in the Ellicotts' dining-room—the butter was only brought in a little while ago, but already it is yellow mush. There are little drops on the backs of Mr. Ellicott's hands. Oliver wants to help Nancy take away the dishes and bring in the fruit—they have started to make a game out of it already when Mrs. Ellicott's voice enforces order.

"No, Oliver. No, please. Please sit still. It is so seldom we have a *guest* that Nancy and I are apt to forget our *manners*—"

Oliver looks to Nancy for guidance, receives it and subsides into his chair. That's just the trouble, he thinks rather peevishly—if only Mrs. Ellicott would stop acting as if he were a guest—and not exactly a guest by choice at that but one who must be the more scrupulously entertained in public, the less he is liked in private.

The fruit. Mrs. Ellicott apologizing for it—her voice implies that she is quite sure Oliver doesn't think it good enough for him but that he ought to feel himself very lucky indeed that it isn't his deserts instead. Mr. Ellicott absent-mindedly squirting orange juice up his sleeve. Oliver and Nancy looking at each other.

"Are you the same?" say both kinds of eyes, intent, absorbed with the wish that has been starved small through the last three months, but now grows again like a smoke-tree out of a magicked jar, "Really the same and really loving me and really glad to be here?" But they can get no proper sort of answer now—there are too many other Ellicotts around, especially

Mrs. Ellicott.

Dinner is over with coffee and cigarettes that Mrs. Ellicott has bought for Oliver because no one shall ever say she failed in the smallest punctilio of hospitality, though she offers them to him with a gesture like that of a missionary returning his baked-mud idol to a Bushman too far gone in sin to reclaim. Mr. Ellicott smoked cigarettes before his marriage. For twenty years now he has been a contributing member of the Anti-Tobacco League.

And now all that Oliver knows is that unless he can talk to Nancy soon and alone, he will start being very rude. It is not that he wants to be rude—especially to Nancy's family—but the impulse to get everyone but Nancy away by any means from sarcasm to homicidal mania is as reasonless and strong as the wish to be born. After all he and Nancy have not seen each other wakingly for three months—and there is still her "grand news" to tell, the grandness of which has seemed to grow more and more dubious the longer she looked at Oliver. Now is the time for Mr. and Mrs. Ellicott to disappear as casually and completely as clouds over the edge of the sky and first of all, not to mention the fact that they are going. But Mrs. Ellicott has far too much tact ever to be understanding.

She puts Mr. Ellicott's hat on for him and takes his arm as firmly as if she were police, and he accepts the grasp with the meekness of an old offender who is not quite sure what particular crime he is being arrested for this time but has an uncomfortable knowledge that it may be any one of a dozen.

"Now we old people are going to leave you, children alone for a little while" she announces, fair to the last, her voice sweeter than ever. "We know you have such a great many important *affairs* to talk over—particularly the *splendid* offer that has just come to Nancy—my little girl hasn't told you about it yet, has she, Oliver?'

"No, Mrs. Ellicott."

"Well, her father and myself consider it quite *remarkable* and we have been *urging*—very *strongly*—her acceptance, though of course" this with a glace smile, "we realize that we are only her *parents*. And, as Nancy knows, it has always been our dearest wish to have her decide matters affecting her happiness entirely *herself.* But I feel sure that when both of you have talked it *well* over, we can trust you both to come to a most *reasonable* decision." She breathes heavily and moves with her appurtenance to the door, secure as an ostrich in the belief that Oliver thinks her impartial, even affectionate. Her conscientiousness gives her a good deal of applause for leaving the two young people so soon when they have all one evening and another morning to be together—but subconsciously she knows that she has done her best by her recent little speech to make this talking-it-over a walk through a field full of small pestilent burrs, for both Oliver and Nancy. They say *au revoir* very politely—all four—the door shuts on Mr. Ellicott's meek back.

Mrs. Ellicott is not very happy, going downstairs. She knows what has undoubtedly happened the moment the door was shut—and a little twinge of something very like the taste of sour grapes goes through her as she thinks of those two young people so reprehensibly glad at being even for the moment in each other's arms.

XIV

An hour later and still the grand news hasn't been told. In fact very little that Mrs. Ellicott would regard as either sensible or reasonable has happened at all. Though they do not know it the conversation has been oddly like that of two dried desert-travellers who have suddenly come upon water and for quite a while afterwards find it hard to think of anything else. But finally:

"Dearest, dearest, what was the grand news?" says Oliver half-drowsily. "We must talk it over, dear, I suppose, I guess, oh, we must—oh, but you're so sweet—" and he relapses again into speechlessness.

They are close together, he and she now. Their lips meet—and meet—with a sweet touch—with a long pressure—children being good to each other—cloud mingling with gleaming cloud.

"Ollie dear." Nancy's voice comes from somewhere as far away and still as if she were talking out of a star. "Stop kissing me. I can't think when you kiss me, I can only feel you be close. If you want to hear about that news, that is," she adds, her lips hardly moving.

All that Oliver wants to do is to hold her and be quiet—to make out of the stuffy room, the nervous rushing of noise under the window, the air exhausted with heat, a place in some measure peaceful, in some measure retired, where they can lie under lucent peace for a moment as shells lie in clear water and not be worried about anything any more. But again, the time they are to have is too short—Oliver really must be back Monday afternoon—already he is unpleasantly conscious of the time-table part of his mind talking trains at him. He takes his arms from around Nancy—she sits up rubbing her eyes with the back of her hand as if to take the dream that was so glittering in them away now she and Oliver have to talk business-affairs.

"Oh, my *hair*—lucky it's bobbed, that's all—I'd have lost all the hairpins I ever had in it by now—Well, Ollie—"

Her hand goes over to his uneasily, takes hold. For a moment the dream comes back and she forgets entirely what she was going to say.

"Oh *dear*!"

"Nancy, Nancy, Nancy!"

But she will be firm about their talking. "No, we mustn't really, we mustn't, or I can't tell you anything at all. Well, it's this.

"I didn't tell you about it at all—didn't even imagine it would come to anything. But that old geology specimen Mrs. Winters knows the art-editor of "The Bazaar" and she happened to say so once when she was here being gloomy with mother, so I wormed a letter out of her to her friend about me. And I sent some things in and the poor man seemed to be interested—at least he said he wanted to see more—and then we started having a real correspondence. Until finally—it was that Friday because I wrote you the letter right away—he goes and sends me a letter saying to come on to New York—that I can have a regular job with them if I want to, and if they like my stuff well enough, after a couple of months they'll send me to Paris to do fashions over there and pay me a salary I can more than live on and everything!"

Nancy cannot help ending with a good deal of triumph, though there is anxiety behind the triumph as well. But to Oliver it seems as if the floor had come apart under his feet.

When he has failed so ludicrously and completely, Nancy has succeeded and succeeded beyond even his own ideas of success. She can go to Paris and have all they ever planned together, now; it has all bent down to her like an apple on a swinging bough, all hers to take, from lunch at Prunier's and sunset over the river to that perfect little apartment they know every window of by heart—and he is no nearer it than he was eight months ago. He has felt the pride in her voice and knows it as most human and justified, but because he is young and unreasonable that pride of hers hurts his own. And then there is something else. All through what she was saying it was "I" that said, not "we."

"That's fine, Nancy," he says uncertainly. "That's certainly fine!"

But she knows by his voice in a second.

"Oh, Ollie, Ollie, of course I won't take it if it makes you feel that way, dear. Why, I wouldn't do anything that would hurt you—but Ollie I don't see how this can, how this could change things any way at all. I only thought it would bring things nearer—both of us getting jobs and my having a Paris one and—"

Her voice might be anything else in the world, but it is not wholly convinced. And its being sure beyond bounds is the only thing that could possibly help Oliver. He puts his hands on her shoulders.

"I couldn't do anything but tell you to take it, dearest, could I? When it's such a real chance?" He is hoping with illogical but none the less painful desperation that she will deny him. But she nods instead.

"Well then, Nancy dear, listen. If you take it, we've got to face things, haven't we?"

She nods a little rebelliously.

"But why is it so *serious*, Ollie?" and again her voice is not true.

"You know. Because I've failed—God knows when I'll make enough money for us to get married now—with the novel gone bust and everything. And I haven't any right to keep you like this when I'm not sure of ever being able to marry you— and when you've got a job like this and can go right ahead on the things you've always been crazy to do. Nancy, you *want* to take it—even if it meant our not getting married for another year and your being away—don't you, don't you? Oh, Nancy, you've *got* to tell me—it'll only bust everything we've had already if you don't!"

And now they have come to a point of misunderstanding that only a trust as unreasonable as belief in immortality will help. But that trust could never be bothered with the truth of what it was saying at the moment—it would have to reach into something deeper than any transitory feeling—and they have an unlucky tradition of always trying to tell each other what is exactly true. And so Nancy nods because she has to, though she couldn't bear to put what that means into words.

"Well, you take it. And I'm awful sorry we couldn't make it go, dear. I tried as hard as I could to make it go but I guess I didn't have the stuff, that's all."

He has risen now and his face seems curiously twisted— twisted as if something hot and hurtful had passed over it and left it so that it would always look that way. He can hardly bear to look at Nancy, but she has risen and started talking hurriedly—fright, amazement, concern and a queer little touch of relief all mixing in her voice.

"But Ollie, if you can't *trust* me about something as little as that."

"It isn't that," he says beatenly and she knows it isn't. And knowing, her voice becomes suddenly frightened—the fright of a child who has let something as fragile and precious as a vessel of golden glass slip out of her hands.

"But, Ollie dear! But, Ollie, I never meant it that way. But Ollie, I love you!"

He takes her in his arms again and they kiss long. This time though there is no peace in the kiss, only the lost passion of bodies tired beyond speech. "Do you love me, Nancy?"

Again she has to decide—and the truth that will not matter for more than the hour wins. Besides, he has hurt her.

"Oh, Ollie, Ollie, yes, but—"

"You're not sure any more?"

"It's different."

"It's not being certain?"

"Not the way it was at first—but, Ollie, we're neither of us the same—"

"Then you *aren't* sure?"

"I can't—I haven't—oh, Ollie, I don't know, I don't know!"

"That means you know."

Again the kiss but this time their lips only hurt against each other—Oliver feels for a ghastly instant as if he were kissing Nancy after she had died. It seems to him that everything in him has made itself into a question as discordant and unanswered as the tearing cry of a puppy baying the moon, struck out of his senses by that swimming round silver above him, ineffably lustrous, ineffably removed, none of it ever coming to touch him but light too pale to help at all. He is holding a girl in his arms—he can feel her body against him—but it is not Nancy he is holding—it never will be Nancy any more. He releases her and starts walking up and down in a series of short, uneasy strides, turning mechanically to keep out of the way of chairs. Words come out of him, words he never imagined he could ever say, he thinks dizzily that it would feel like this if he were invisibly bleeding to death—that would come the same way in fiery spurts and pauses that tore at the body.

"Don't you see, dear, don't you *see*? It's been eight months now and we aren't any nearer getting married than we were at first and it isn't honest to say we will be soon any more—I can't see any prospect—I've failed in everything I thought would go—and we can't get married on my job for *years*—I'm not good enough at it—and I *won't* have you hurt—I *won't* have you tied to me when it only means neither of us doing what we want and both of us getting, older and our work not done. Oh, I love you, Nancy—if there was any hope at all I'd go down on my knees to ask you to keep on but there isn't—they've beaten us—they've beaten us—all the fat old people who told us we were too poor and too young. All we do is go on like this both of us getting worked up whenever we see each other and both of us hurting each other and nothing happening—Oh, Nancy, I thought we could help each other always and now we can't even a little any more. You remember when we promised that if either of us stopping loving each other we'd tell?"

Nancy is very silent and rather white.

"Yes, Ollie."

"Well, Nancy?"

"Well—"

They look at each other as if they were watching each other burn.

"Good-by darling, darling, darling!" says Ollie through lips like a marionette's.

Then Nancy feels him take hold of her again—the arms of somebody else in Oliver's body—and a cold mouth hurting her cheek—and still she cannot speak. And then the queer man who was walking up and down so disturbingly has gone out of the door.

XV

Oliver finds himself walking along a long street in a city. It is not a distinguished street by any means—there are neither plate-glass shops nor 'residences' on it—just an ordinary street of little stores and small houses and occasionally an apartment building named for a Pullman car. In a good many houses the lights are out already—it is nearly eleven o'clock and this part of St. Louis goes to bed early—only the drugstores and the moving-picture theatres are still flaringly awake. His eyes read the sign that he passes mechanically, "Dr. Edwin K. Buffinton—Chiropractor," "McMurphy and Kane's," "The Rossiter," with its pillars that look as if they had been molded out of marbled soap.

Thought. Memory. Pain. Pain pressing down on his eyeballs like an iron thumb, twisting wires around his forehead tighter and tighter till it's funny the people he passes don't see the patterns they make on his skin.

Somebody talking in his mind, quite steadily and flatly, repeating and repeating itself like a piece of cheap music played over and over again on a scratched phonograph record, talking in the voice that is a composite of a dozen voices; a fat man comfortable on a club lounge laying down the law as if he were carefully smearing the shine out of something brilliant with a flaccid heavy finger; a thin sour woman telling children playing together "don't, don't, don't," in the whine of a nasty nurse.

"All for the best, you know—all for the best, we're all of us sure of that. Love doesn't last—doesn't last—doesn't last—as good fish in the sea as ever were caught out of it—nobody's heart could break at twenty-five. You think you're happy and proud—you think you're lovers and friends—but that doesn't last, doesn't last, doesn't last—none of it lasts at all."

If he only weren't so *tired* he could do something. But instead he feels only as a man feels who has been drinking all day in the instant before complete intoxication—his body is as distinct from him as if it were walking behind him with his shadow—all the colors he sees seem exaggeratedly dull or brilliant, he has little sense of distance, the next street corner may be a block or a mile away, it is all the same, his feet will take him there, his feet that keep going mechanically, one after the other, one after the other, as if they marched to a clock. There is no feeling in him that stays long enough to be called by any definite word—there is only a streaming parade of sensations like blind men running through mist, shapes that come out of fog and sink back to it, without sight, without number, without name, with only continual hurry of feet to tell of their presence.

A slinky man comes up at his elbow and starts to talk out of the side of his mouth.

"Say, mister—"

"Oh, *go* to hell!" and the man fades away again, without even looking startled, to mutter "Well, you needn' be so damn peeved about it—I'll say you needn' be so damn peeved— whatcha think you are, anyhow—Marathon Mike?" as Oliver's feet take Oliver swiftly away from him.

Nancy. The first time he ever kissed her when it was question and answer with neither of them sure. And then getting surer and surer—and then when they kissed. Never touching Nancy, never. Never seeing her again never any more. That song the Glee Club used to harmonize over—what was it?

Stephen Vincent Benet

We won't go there any more,
We won't go there any more
We won't go there any mo-o-ore—

He lifts his eyes for a moment. A large blue policeman is looking at him fixedly from the other side of the street, his nightstick twirling in a very prepared sort of way. For an instant Oliver sees himself going over and asking that policeman for his helmet to play with. That would be the cream of the jest—the very cream—to end the evening in combat with a large blue policeman after having all you wanted in life break under you suddenly like new ice.

He had been walking for a very long time. He ought to go to bed. He had a hotel somewhere if he could only think where. The policeman might know.

The policeman saw a young man with staring eyes coming toward him, remarked "hophead" internally and played with his nightstick a little more. The nearer Oliver came the larger and more unsympathetic the policeman seemed to him. Still, if you couldn't remember what your hotel was yourself it was only sensible to ask guidance on the question. His mind reacted suddenly toward grotesqueness. One had to be very polite to large policemen. The politeness should, naturally, increase as the square of the policeman.

"I wonder if you could tell me where my hotel is, officer?" Oliver began. "What hotel?" said the policeman uninterestedly. Oliver noticed with an inane distinctness that he had started to swirl his nightstick as a large blue cat might switch its tail. He wondered if it would be tactful to ask him if he had ever been a drum major. Then he realized that the policeman had asked him a question—courtesy demanded a prompt response.

"What?" said Oliver.

"I said 'What hotel?'" The policeman was beginning to

be annoyed.

Oliver started to think of his hotel. It was imbecile not to remember the name of your own hotel—even when your own particular material and immaterial cosmos had been telescoped like a toy train in the last three hours. The Rossiter was all that he could think of.

"The Rossiter," he said firmly.

"No hotel Rossiter in *this* town." The policeman's nightstick was getting more and more irritated. "Rossiter's a lotta flats. You live there?"

"No. I live in a hotel."

"Well, what hotel?"

"Oh, I tell you I don't remember," said Oliver vaguely. "A big one with a lot of electric lights."

The policeman's face became suddenly very red.

"Well, you move on, buddy!" he said in a tone of hoarse displeasure. "You move right on! You don't come around me with any of your funny cracks—I know whatsa matter with you, all right, all right. I know whatsa matter with you."

"So do I." Oliver was smiling a little now, the whole scene was so arabesque. "I want to go to my hotel."

"You move on. You move on *quick*!" said the policeman vastly. "It's a long walk down to the hoosegow and *I* don't want to take you there."

"I don't want to go there," said Oliver. "But my hotel—"

"*Quit arguin'*"! said the policeman in a bark like a teased bulldog.

Oliver turned and walked two steps away. Then he turned again. After all why not? The important part of his life was over anyhow—and before the rest of it finished he might be able to tell one large policeman just what he thought of him.

"Why, you big blue boob," he began abruptly with a sense of pleasant refreshment better than drink, "You great heaving purple ice wagon—" and then he was stopped abruptly for the policeman was taking the necessary breath away.

XVI

About which time Nancy had finished crying—raging at herself all the time, she hated to cry so—and was sitting up straight on the couch looking at the door which Oliver had shut as if by looking it very hard indeed she could make it turn into Oliver.

It *couldn't* end this way. If it did it just meant that all the last year wasn't real—hadn't any more part in reality than charity theatricals. And they'd both of them been so sure that it was the chief reality that they had ever known.

He wasn't *reasonable*. She hadn't wanted the darned old job, she'd wanted to marry him, but as long as they hadn't seemed to get very far in the last eight months when he'd been trying to work it—why couldn't *she* try—

Then 'Oh Nancy, be honest!' to herself. No, that wasn't true. She'd wanted the job, wanted to get it, hadn't thought about Oliver particularly when she'd tried for it except to be a little impatient with him for not using more judgment when he picked out his job. Did that mean that she didn't love him? Oh Lord, it was all so mixed up.

Starting out so clearly at first and everything being so perfect— and then the last four months and both getting tireder and tireder and all the useless little misunderstandings that made you wonder how could you if you really cared. And now this.

Stephen Vincent Benet

For an instant of mere relief from strain Nancy saw herself in Paris, studying as she had always wanted to study, doing some real work, all Paris hers to play with like a big gray stone toy, never having to worry about loving, about being loved, about people you loved. Being free. Like taking off your hot, hot clothes and lying in water when you were too hot and tired even to think of sleeping. Oliver too—she'd leave him free— he'd really work better without her—without having her to take care of and make money for and worry about always—

The mind turned the other way. But what would doing anything be like with Oliver out of it when doing things together had been all that mattered all the last year?

They couldn't decide things like this on a prickly hot August night when both of them were nearly dead with fatigue. It wasn't *real*. Even after Oliver had shut the door she'd been sure he'd come back, though she hoped he wouldn't just while she was crying; she never had been, she thought viciously, one of those happy people who look like rain-goddesses when they cry.

He must come back. She shut her eyes and told him to as hard as she could. But he didn't.

All very well to be proud and dignified when both of you lived near each other. But Oliver was going back to New York tomorrow—and if he went back while they were still like this—She knew his train—the ten seven.

She tried being proud in a dozen different expressive attitudes for ten minutes or so: Then she suddenly relaxed and went over to the telephone, smiling rather ashamedly at herself.

"Hotel Rosario?"

"Yes."

"Can I speak to Mr. Oliver Crowe? He is staying there

isn't he?"

A pause full of little jingling sounds.

"Yes, he's staying here but he hasn't come in yet this evening. Do you wish to leave a message?"

Nancy hesitates.

"N-no." That would be just a little too humble.

"Or the name of the party calling?" He will know, of course. Still, had she better say? Then she remembers the need of punishing him just a little. After all—it is hardly fair she should go all the way toward making up when he hasn't even started.

"No—no name. But tell him somebody called, please."

"Very well."

And Nancy goes back to wonder if the reason Oliver hasn't gone back to the hotel is that he is returning here in an appropriate suit of sackcloth. She hopes he *will* come before mother and father get back.

But even while she is hoping it, the large blue policeman is saying something about "Sturbance of the peace" to the desk-sergeant, and Oliver is going down on the blotter as Donald Richardson.

XVII

"You simply must not worry yourself about it so, Nancy, my darling," says Mrs. Ellicott brightly. "Lovers' quarrels are only lovers' quarrels you know and they seem very small indeed to people a little older and more experienced though I daresay they may loom terribly large just at present. Why your father and myself used to have—ahem—our little times over *trifles*, darling, mere *trifles* " and Mrs. Ellicott takes a pinch of air between finger and thumb as if to display it as a specimen of those mere trifles over which Mr. and Mrs. Ellicott used to become proudly enraged at each other in the days before she had faded him so completely.

Nancy, after a night of intensive sleeplessness broken only by dreams of seeing Oliver being married to somebody else in the lobby of the Hotel Rosario can only wonder rather dully when it could ever have been that poor father was allowed enough initiative of his own to take even the passive part in a quarrel over a trifle and why mother thinks the prospect implied in her speech of her daughter's marriage being like unto hers can be so comforting. Nancy made one New Year's resolution the second day of her engagement, "If I ever find myself starting to act to Ollie the way mother does to father I'll simply have to leave him and never see him again." But Mrs. Ellicott goes on.

"If Oliver is at all the sort of young man we must hope he is, he will certainly come and apologize at once. And if he should not—well Nancy, my little girl," she adds hieroglyphically "there are many trials that seem hard to bear at first which prove true blessings later when we see of what false materials they were first composed."

Mr. Ellicott thinks it is time for him to go to the office. It is five minutes ahead of his usual time but Mrs. Ellicott has been looking at him all the way through her last speech until he feels uneasily that he must be composed of very false material indeed. He stops first though to give an ineffective pat to Nancy's shoulder.

"Cheer up, Chick," he says kindly. "Always sun somewhere you know, so don't treat the poor boy too hard," and he shuffles rapidly away before his wife can look all the way through him for the vague heresy implicit in his sentence.

"It is all very well for your father to say such things, but, Nancy, darling, you shall not be put upon by Tramplers" proceeds Mrs. Ellicott in her most cryptically perfect tones. "Oliver is a man—he must apologize. A man, I say, though little more than a boy. And otherwise you would now be pursuing your Art in Paris due to dear kind Mrs. Winters who has always stood our truest friend and now this other opportunity has come also but I would never be the first to say that even such should not be sacrificed most gladly for the love of a true kind husband and dear little children though marriage is but a lottery at best and especially when affections are fixed upon their object in early youth."

All this without a pause, pouring over the numbed parts of Nancy's mind like thin sweetish oil. Nancy considers wearily. Yes, Oliver should apologize. Yes, it is only being properly dignified not to call up the Rosario again to find if he is there. Yes, if he truly loves her, he will call—he will come—and the clock hands are marching on toward ten-seven and his train like stiff little soldiers and mother is talking, talking—

"Not that I wish or have wished to influence your mind in any way, my darling, but environment and propinquity count for mountains in such first youthful attachments and sometimes when we are older to be looked back upon with such regret. Nor would I ever have Words Spoken that should seem to injure the choice of my daughter's heart—but when young men cannot provide even Hovels for their *fiancees* a reasonable time having been given, it is only just that they should release them and you looking like death all these last two months. Never wishing that my own daughter should act in Ways dishonorable in the slightest but time is the Test in such matters and if such tests are not to be survived it is best they should end and no one can deny that the young man talks very queerly and was often quite disrespectful to you though you may say that was joking but it would not have been joking in my day and young men with queer nervous eyes and hands I never have nor will quite trust—"

But it's Oliver that's doing this, Oliver who turned funny and white when she cut her finger with the breadknife making sandwiches and wanted her to put all sorts of things on it. Oliver who was always so sweet when she was unreasonable and always the first to come looking unhappy after they'd quarrelled even a little and say it was all his fault. Why the very last letter she got from him was the one that said if she ever stopped loving him he knew he'd die.

"And when things are ended it is better that such things should be though doubtless not necessary to put an announcement in the paper yet since God in his infinite wisdom arranges all things for the best. And with such a splendid position opening before her it would be only dignified to bring the young man to his senses for it would not be right to let unreasonable young men stand in the way of advantages offered by Foreign Travel and study and these things are soon forgotten, my dear, and if nervous young men will not admit like gentlemen that they are in the wrong when only engaged what kind of husbands will they make when married forever? And is not a broken engagement better than lifelong unhappiness when there are so many too many sinful people divorcing each other every day and all men who write for their living use stimulants, my dear, such is literary history and my dearest have your cry out on mother's shoulder."

The sweetish oil has risen about Nancy relentlessly—it is up to her waist now and still it keeps talking and flowing and creeping higher. Very soon when the fatter black soldier on the clock-face has only hitched himself along a little, it will be over her head and the roving Nancy, the sparkling Nancy, the Nancy that fell in love will be under it like a calm body, never to rise or run or be kissed with light seeking kisses on the soft of her throat again. There will only be a dignified Nancy, a sensible Nancy, a Nancy going to Paris to study and be successful, a Nancy who, sooner or later will marry "Some good, clean man."

A little tinkle of chimes from the clock. Six minutes more. The Nancy that was stands on tiptoe, every eager and tameless bit of her hoping, hoping. If mother weren't there that Nancy would have been at the telephone an hour ago in spite of young people's pride and old people's self-respect and all the thousand and one knife-faced fetishes that all the correct and common-sensible people hug close and worship because they hurt.

She can see the train sliding out of the station. Ollie is in it and his face is stiff with surprise and unforgiveness like the face of some horrible stranger you went up to and spoke to by mistake, thinking he was your friend. By the time the train is well started he will have begun talking to that fluffy girl in the other half of the Pullman—no, that isn't worthy, he wouldn't—but oh Ollie, Ollie!

Half an hour later the telephone rings. Nancy is finishing the breakfast dishes—her hands jump as she hears it—a slippery plate slops back into the water and as she dives after it she realizes painfully that the new water is much too hot.

"What *is* it, mother?" For an instant the Nancy who has no real self- respect is talking again.

"Just a minute, Isabella. Mrs. Winters, dear. Don't you want to speak to her?"

"Oh."

Then—

"Not right now. When I'm through with these. But will you ask her if she's going to be in this afternoon—I want to tell her about my taking the New York job."

Satisfied oil pouring back into the telephone with a pleased, thin chuckle.

"Yes, Nancy has decided. Well, dear, I think she had better tell you herself—"

Nancy is looking dolefully down at her thumb. Foolish not to have cooled off that water a little—she has really burned herself. For an instant she hears Oliver's voice in her ears, low and concerned, sees Oliver kissing it, making it well. But these things don't happen to sensible, self-respecting modern girls with experienced mothers, especially when all the former have now quite made up their own minds.

XVIII

It was with some nightmare surprise that Oliver on waking regarded his tidy cell. Then he remembered and in spite of the fact that yesterday evening with all that belonged to it kept hurting wherever it was that most of him lived with the stiff repeating ache of a nerve struck again and again by the same soft hammer, he couldn't help laughing a little. The popular college remedy for disprized love had always been an instantaneous mingling of conflicting alcohols—calling a large policeman a big blue boob seemed to produce the same desired result of bringing one to one's senses by first taking one completely out of them without the revolving stomach and fuzzed mind of the first instance. He tried to think of yesterday evening airily. Silly children quarreling about things that didn't matter at all. Of course Nancy should have the job if she wanted—of course he'd apologize, apologize like Ecclesiastes even for being alive at all if it was necessary—and then everything would be *all* right, just all right and fixed. But the airy attitude somehow failed to comfort—it was a little too much like trying to shuffle a soft-shoe clog on a new grave. Nancy *had* been unreasonable. Nancy *had* said or hadn't denied that she wasn't sure she loved him any more. He *had* released her from the engagement and told her good-by. He stared at the facts—they sprang up in front of him like choking thorns—thorns he had to clear away with his hands before he could even touch Nancy again. Was he sure—even now? All the airiness dropped from him like a clown's false face. As he thought of what would happen if Nancy had really meant it about not loving him, it seemed to him that

Stephen Vincent Benet

somebody had taken away the pit of his stomach and left nothing in its place but air.

Anyhow the first thing to do was to get out of this place—he examined the neat bars in the door approvingly and wondered how the devil you acted when you wanted to be let out. There wasn't any way of opening a conversation about it with no one to talk to—and the corridor was merely a length of empty steel—and, damn it, his train left at Ten Seven and he had to see Nancy and explain everything in the world before it left— and if he didn't get back to New York in time he might lose his job. There must be some way of explaining to the people in charge that he hadn't done anything but kid a policeman— that he must get out.

He went over to the door and tried it tentatively—no inside doorknob, of course, this wasn't a hotel. He looked through the bars—nothing but corridor and the cell on the other side. Should he call? For an instant the fantastic idea of crying "Waiter!" or "Please send up my breakfast!" tugged at him hard, but fantasy had got him into much too much trouble as it was, he reflected savagely. It made you feel ridiculously self-conscious, standing behind bars like this and shouting into emptiness. Still he had to get out. He cleared his throat.

"Hey," he remarked in a pleasant conversational tone. "Hey!"

No answer, he grew bolder.

"Hey!" This time the conversational tone was italicized. A rustle of voices somewhere rewarded him—that must be people talking. Well, if they talked, they could listen.

"HEY!" and now his voice was emphatic enough for headline capitals.

The rustle of voices ceased. There was a moment of stupefied silence. Then,

"SHUT UP!" came from the end of the corridor in a roar that made Oliver feel as if he had been cooing. The roar irritated him—they might be a little more mannerly. He clutched the bars and discovered to his pleased surprise that they would rattle. He shook them as hard as he could like a monkey asking for peanuts.

"Hey there! I want to get out!" and though he tried to make his voice as impressive as possible it seemed to him to pipe like a canary's in that long steel emptiness.

"I've got to catch a train!" he added desperately and then had to stuff his coat sleeve into his mouth to keep from spoiling his dramatics with most unseasonable mirth.

There were noises from the end of the corridor—the noises of strong men at bitter war with something stronger than they, strange rumblings and snortings and muffled whoops. Then the voice came again and this time its words were slow and deliberately spaced so as to give it time to master whatever rocked it between whiles.

"Say—you—*humorist*" said the voice and here it rose sharply into an undignified squawk of laughter, "You—innercent— child—comedian—you—Charlie—Chaplin—of the—hoose- gow—you *shut* up—or I'll come down there and—bend— something—over—your merry little face—*understand?*" "Yes sir," said Oliver subduedly.

"Ah right. Now go bye-bye—mama'll call you when she's ready to take you walking" then explosively "I got to catch a train! Oh Holy Mike!"

Oliver left the window and went back toward his bunk, considerably chastened. As he did so a bundle of second-hand clothes on the floor rolled over and disclosed a red and unshaven face.

"Wup!" said Oliver—he had almost stepped on it.

Stephen Vincent Benet

"Wha'?" said the bundle, opening sick eyes.

"Oh nothing. I only said good morning."

"Wha'?"

"Good morning."

"Wha'?"

"Good morning."

After incredible difficulties, the bundle attained a sitting position.

"You kid'n me?" it demanded thickly, looking at Oliver with as much surprise as if he had just grown up out of the floor like a plant.

"Oh no. No."

"You're *nah* kid'n me?"

"No."

"Ah ri'. 'S countersign. Pass. Fren'."

It attempted a military gesture but succeeded merely in hitting its mouth with its hand. It then looked at the hand as if the latter had done it on purpose and became sunk in profound cogitation.

"Not feeling very well today?" Oliver ventured.

It looked at him.

"*Well?*" it said briefly. Then, after a silence devoted to trying to find where its hands were.

"Hoosh."

"What?" said Oliver.

"*Hoosh*. Goo' hoosh. Gran' hoosh. Oh, *hoosh!*" and as if the mention of the word had stricken it back into clothes again it slid slowly down on its back, closed its eyes and began to snore.

Oliver, perched on his bunk for what comfort there was, sat and considered. He looked at the bundle—the bars—the bars—the bundle. The bundle wheezed apoplectically—no sound of footsteps came from beyond the bars. Oliver wondered if Nancy loved him. He wondered if he would ever catch that Ten Seven. But most of all he wondered why on earth he had happened to get in here and how on earth he was ever going to get out.

XIX

The sky had been a blue steam all day, but at night it quieted, there were faint airs. From the window of the apartment on Riverside Drive you could see it grow gentle, fade from a strong heat of azure through gray gauze into darkness, thick-soft as a sable's fur at first, then uneasily patterned all at once with idle leopard-spottings and strokes of light. The lights fell into the river and dissolved, the dark wash took them and carried them into streaks of lesser, more fluid light. Even so, if there could have been country silence for five minutes at a time, the running river, the hills so disturbed with light beyond, might have worn some aspect of peace. But even in the high bird's nest of the apartment there was no real silence, only a pretending at silence, like the forced quiet of a child told to keep still in a corner—the two people dining together could talk in whispers, if they wanted, and still be heard, but always at the back of the brain of either ran a thin pulsation of mumbling sound like the buzz of a kettle-drum softly struck in a passage of music where the orchestra talks full-voiced—the night sound of the city, breathing and moving and saying words.

They must have been married rather contentedly for quite a while now, they said so little of importance at dinner and yet seemed so quietly pleased at having dinner together and so neat at understanding half sentences without asking explanations. That would have been the first conclusion of anybody who had been able to take out a wall and watch their doll-house unobserved. Besides, though the short, decided man with the greyish hair must be fifty at least, the woman who stood his own height when she rose from the table was too slimly mature for anything but the thirties. Not a highly original New York couple by any means—a prospering banker or president of a Consolidated Toothpick Company with a beautiful wife, American matron-without-children model, except for her chin which was less dimpled than cleft with decisiveness and the wholly original lustre of her hair, a buried lustre like the shine of "Murray's red gold" in a Border ballad. A wife rather less society-stricken than the run of such wives since she obviously preferred hot August in a New York apartment with her husband's company to beach-picnics at Greenwich or Southampton without it. Still the apartment, though compact as an army mess-kit, was perfectly furnished and the maid who had served the cool little dinner an efficient effacedness of the race that housekeepers with large families and little money assert passed with the Spanish War. Money enough, and the knowledge of how to use it without blatancy or pinching—that would have been the second conclusion.

They were sitting in deep chairs in the living room now, a tall-stemmed reading lamp glowing softly between them, hardly speaking. The tiredness that had been in the man's face like the writing in a 'crossed' letter began to leave it softly. He reached over, took the woman's hand and held it—not closely or with greediness but with a firm clasp that had something weary like appeal in it and something strong like a knowledge of rest.

"Always like this, at home," he said slowly.

"It *is* rather sweet." Her voice had the gentleness of water running into water. Her eyes looked at him once and left him deliberately but not as if they didn't care. It must have been a love-match in the beginning then—her eyes seemed so infirm.

"You'll read a little?"

"Yes."

Stephen Vincent Benet

"Home," he said. He seemed queerly satisfied to say the word, queerly moved as if even after so much reality had been lived through together, he couldn't quite believe that it was reality.

"And I've been waiting for it—five days, six days, this time?"

She must have been at the seashore after all—tan or lack of it meant little these days, especially to a woman who lived in this kind of an apartment. The third conclusion might have been rather sentimental, a title out of a moving picture—something about Even in the Wastes of the Giant City the Weary Heart Will Always Turn To—Just Home.

A doll on a small table began to buzz mysteriously in its internals. The man released the woman's hand—both looking deeply annoyed.

"I thought we had a private number here," said the man, the tiredness coming back into his face like scribbles on parchment.

She crossed to the telephone with a charming furtiveness—you could see she was playing they had just been found behind the piano together in a game of hide-and-seek. The doll was disembowelled of its telephone.

"No—No—Oh very well—"

"What was it?"

She smiled.

"Is this the Eclair Picture Palace?" she mimicked. Both seemed almost childishly relieved. So in spite of his successful-business-man mouth, he wasn't the kind that is less a husband than a telephone-receiver, especially at home. Still, she would have made a difference even to telephone-receivers, that could be felt even without the usual complement of senses.

"That was—bothersome for a minute." His tone lent the words a quaint accent of scare.

"Oh, well—if you have one at all—the way the service is now—"

"There won't be any telephone when we take our vacation together, that's *settled*."

She had been kneeling, examining a bookcase for books. Now she turned with one in her hand, her hair ruddy and smooth as ruddy amber in the reflected light.

"No, but *telegrams*. And wireless," she whispered mockingly, the more mockingly because it so obviously made him worried as a worried boy. She came over and stood smoothing his ear a moment, a half-unconscious customary gesture, no doubt, for he relaxed under it and the look of rest came back. Then she went to her chair, sat down and opened the book.

"No use borrowing trouble now, dear. Now listen. Cigar?"
"Going."

"Ashtray?"

"Yes."

"And remember not to knock it over when you get excited. Promise?"

"Um."

"Very well."

Mrs. Severance's even voice began to flow into the stillness.

"As I was getting too big for Mr. Wopsle's great-aunt—"

XX

"And that's the end of the chapter." Mrs. Severance's voice trailed off into silence. She closed the book with a soft sound. The man whom it might be rather more convenient than otherwise to call Mr. Severance opened his eyes. He had not been asleep, but he had found by a good deal of experience that he paid more attention to Dickens if he closed his eyes while she read.

"Thank you dear."

"Thank you. You know I love it. Especially Pip."

He considered.

"There was a word one of my young men used the other day about Dickens. Gusto, I think—yes, that was it. Well, I find that, as I grow older, that seems to be the thing I value rather more than most men of my age. Gusto." He smiled "Though I take it more quietly, perhaps,—than I did when I was young," he added.

"You *are* young" said Mrs. Severance carefully.

"Not really, dear. I can give half-a-dozen youngsters I know four strokes in nine holes and beat them. I can handle the bank in half the time and with half the worry that some of my people take to one department. And for a little while more, Rose, I may be able to satisfy you. But" and he passed a hand lightly over his hair. "It's grey, you know," he ended.

"As if it mattered," said Mrs. Severance, a little pettishly.

"It does matter, Rose." His eyes darkened with memory—with the sort of memory that hurts more to forget than even to remember. "Do you realize that I am sixteen years older than you are?" he said a little hurriedly as if he were trying to scribble the memory over with any kind of words.

"But my dear" and she smiled, "you were sixteen years older six years ago—remember? There's less real difference between us now than there was then."

"Yes, I certainly wasn't as young in some ways—six years ago." He seemed to speak almost as if unconsciously, almost as if the words were being squeezed out of him in sleep by a thing that had pressed for a long time with a steady weight on his mind till the mind must release itself or be broken. "But then nobody could be with you, for a month even, and not feel himself turn younger whether he wanted to or not." "So that's settled." She was trying to carry it lightly, to take the darkness out of his eyes. "And once you've bought our steamer tickets we can leave it all behind at the wharf and by the time we land we'll be so disgracefully young that no one will recognize us— just think—we can keep going back and back till I'm putting my hair up for the first time and you're in little short trousers—and then babies, I suppose and the other side of getting born—" but her voice, for once, turned ineffectually against his centeredness of gaze, that seemed now as if it had turned back on itself for a struggling moment and regarded neither what was nor what might be, but only what was past.

"Six years ago" he said with the same drowsy thoughtfulness. "Well, Rose, I shall always be—most grateful—for those six years."

She started to speak but he checked her.

Stephen Vincent Benet

"I think I would be willing to make a substantial endowment to any Protestant Church that still really believed in hell," he said, "because that was very like hell—six years ago."

Intensity began to come into his voice like a color of darkness, though he still spoke slowly.

"You can stand nearly everything in life but being tired of yourself. And six years ago I was tired—tired to death."

Her hand reached over and touched him medicinally.

"I suppose I had no right" he began again and then stopped. "No, I think the strong man tires less easily but more wholly than the weak one when he does tire. And I was strong enough.

"I'd played a big game, you know. When my father died we hadn't much left but position—and that was going. I don't blame my father—he wasn't a business man—he should have been a literary critic—that little book of essays of his still sells, you know; not much but there's a demand for a dozen copies every year and that's a good deal for an American who's been dead for thirty. Well, that's where the children get their liking for things like that—I've got it too, a little—I could have done something there if I'd had time. But I never had time.

"I could have done it when I got out of Harvard—drifted along like half a dozen people I know, played at law, played at writing, played always and forever at being a gentleman— ended up as an officer of the Century Club with what little money I had in an annuity. But I couldn't stand the idea of just scraping along. And for nearly ten years I put those things aside.

"You know about my going West and the way I lived there. It wasn't easy when I'd been at Harvard and gone everywhere in New York and Boston—starting in so far below the bottom that you couldn't even see the bottom unless you squinted your eyes. But I never took a job with more money if I thought I could learn anything in a job with less—and every place I went I stayed until I could handle the job of the man two places ahead of me—and if I didn't get his job when I asked for it I went somewhere else. I don't think I read a book except a technical one for the first five years. And after that, when the chain-stores started going they asked me back to New York—a big offer too—but it wasn't the kind I wanted and I threw it down. I knew just how I wanted to come back to New York and that's the way I came.

"I don't suppose my morals were too edifying those years. But they were as good as the men I went with and I kept myself in hand. I saw men go to pieces with drink—and I didn't drink. I saw men go to pieces over women—and I kept away from that kind of woman. A man has to have women in his life no matter how much you talk about it—but I took the kind with the price-tag because when you paid them you were through. I could have married a dozen times if I'd wanted but I didn't want—that old hocus-pocus of tradition was still with me, stronger than death—I thought I knew the kind of wife I wanted and she was in the East.

"Then the partnership with Jessup came and I took it. And after a year I was made. I wasn't the last of one of the penniless old families that give each other dinners once a month and pretend they're the real society because they haven't money enough to trail in the present society game—even by then I was—what did that last newspaper story say? 'a figure of nation-wide importance.' Then it must be just about time, I thought, that this figure of nation-wide importance began to look around a little and married the wife he'd been waiting for and started to pick up all the things he hadn't had for twelve years.

"Well—Mary. And I was so careful about Mary," his lips twisted, half whimsically, half painfully. "I was so damn sure. I was so damn sure I knew everything about women.

Stephen Vincent Benet

"She had the qualities I'd said to myself I wanted—beauty, position, breeding, a good enough mind, some common sense. She hadn't money, but there I thought I could help her—the way she ran things for her father on what they had showed what she could do with more. We weren't in love with each other—oh dear no—but that I considered on the whole an advantage—she attracted me and it's fair enough to say that beside most of the men she'd been seeing my combination of having been Old New York and being one of the young big coming men from the West dazzled her rather. And anyhow I didn't want—passion—exactly. I thought it would take too much time when I was only in the middle of my game and getting as much real solid fun out of it as a kid gets out of cooking his own dinner in camp. I wanted a partner and a home and children and somebody to sit at the head of my table when I wanted to be—public—and yet somebody you could be at home with when you wanted to be at home. And I thought I had them all in Mary—I thought I was being about the most sensible man in the world.

"Well, up till after both children were born I think I tried pretty hard. I gave her all I could think of—materially at least. And then I found out in spite of myself that you can't be married to a woman—even bearably—and neither be lovers nor friends with her. And Mary and I never got beyond the social acquaintance stage.

"It wasn't all Mary's fault either—I can see that now. A good deal was in the way she'd been brought up—they weren't modern about the blisses of ignorance in the nineties. But the rest of it was Mary and she couldn't have changed it any more than she could have been rude to a servant or raised her voice more than usual when she really wanted something done.

"She'd been brought up never to be demonstrative—that was one thing. But that wasn't the main trouble—the main trouble was her most curious, most frigid self-sufficiency. Until her children came she was the most wholly self-sufficient person I've ever known. She was really only happy when she was entirely alone, always. It wasn't egotism exactly—she's always had a very-well-mannered conviction of her own relative unimportance—it was just that in spite of the fact that she seemed so perfectly healthy and calm and composed whenever she was with other people they'd be sure to hurt her a little somehow or other without meaning to—the only person she could genuinely depend on never to hurt her was herself.

"As for men, she'd formed one crystallized opinion of men in the first weeks of our marriage and she's kept it ever since. She looks at them as if they were a kind of tame wolf about the house—something you must never show you're afraid of, something you must feed and look after and be publicly amiable to because you must be just—but something you never never would bring in the house of your own accord or touch without feeling that you, that you had to preserve so jealously against all the things that could possibly hurt it, start to shrink and be pained inside.

"Then the children came—she did and does love them. She lives for them. But they're part of herself too, you see, an essential part, and as she can't give herself to anybody but herself, she can't give them to me even in the easiest kind of partnership, really. You don't leave small children alone with even the tamest kind of wolf—and she's the kind of woman whose children are always six to her. And she's their mother—and so she has her way.

"That's the way it got worse. Right up to six years ago.

"I'd done my job—I was President of the Commercial. And I'd made my money, and the money still kept coming in as if it didn't make any difference what I did with it. I'd won my game. And what was there in it for me?

"I didn't have a home—I had a place where I ate and slept. I didn't have a wife—I had an acquaintance who kept house for me. I had children—at school and college. I didn't have real hobbies—I hadn't had time for them. And I was forty-nine.

Stephen Vincent Benet

All I could do was go on making money till I died.

"Well, you changed that," his voice shook a little.

"You came and I saw and knew and took you. And I'm not sorry. Because you've made me alive again. And I'm going to be alive now till I die.

"Funny—I was never so anxious about anything happening as I have been about—our approaching mutual disappearance. Especially the last six months when I've been planning. But now that's settled.

"Mary will have more than enough and the children are grown. They won't know—I still have brains enough to settle that and money will do nearly everything. It'll be a nine days' wonder. 'Sudden Disappearance of Prominent Financier— Foul Play Suspected' and that'll be all.

"As for the Commercial—I haven't come to my age without finding out that nobody in the world is indispensable. If a taxi ran over me tomorrow they'd have to do without me—and Harris and the young men can handle things.

"But you know where there'll be an elderly gentleman retired from business with a country house and a garden he can putter around in all his worst clothes. And a wife that reads Dickens to him in the evening—oh yes, Rose, we'll take Dickens along. And he'll be pretty contented as things go—that retired old gentleman."

The darkness had passed from his eyes—he was smiling now.

"Be nice—eh Rose?"

He took her hand—the warm touch was still strong, still reassuring. Only the eyes that he was not looking at now seemed singularly unsure, as if they had seen something they had pondered over lightly, as a mere possibility, years ago, take on sudden impatient body and demand to be heard.

She let her hand lie lightly in his for a moment. Then she rose.

"Half past twelve" she said a little stiffly. "Time for two such genuine antiques as we are to think of being put away in our cases for the night."

XXI

It was three in the afternoon before Oliver walked into the Hotel Rosario again and when he did it was with the feeling that the house detective might come up at any moment, touch him quietly on the shoulder and remark that his bag *might* be sent down to the station after him if he paid his bill and left quietly and at once. An appearance before a hoarse judge who fined him ten dollars in as many seconds had not helped his self-confidence though he kept wondering if there was a sliding scale of penalties for improper language applied to the police of St. Louis and just what would have happened if he had called the large blue policeman anything out of his A.E.F. vocabulary. Also the desk, when he called there for his key, reminded him twingingly of the dock, and the clerk behind it looked at him so knowingly as he made the request that Oliver began to construct a hasty moral defence of his whole life from the time he had stolen sugar at eight, when he was reassured by the clerk's merely saying in a voice like a wink. "Telephone call for you last night, Mr. Crowe."

Nancy!

With a horrible effort to keep impassive, "Yes? Who was it?"

"Party didn't leave a name."

"Oh. When?"

"'Bout 'leven o'clock."

"And she didn't leave any message?" Then Oliver turned pink at having betrayed himself so easily.

"No-o—*she* didn't." The clerk's eyelid drooped a trifle. Those college looking boys were certainly hell with women.

"Oh, well—" with a vast attempt to seem careless. "Thanks. Where's the 'phone?"

"Over there" and Oliver followed the direction of the jerked thumb to shut himself up in a booth with his heart, apparently, bent upon doing queer interpretative dances and his mind full of all the most apologetic words in or out of the dictionary. "Hello. Hello. *Is this Nancy?*"

"This is Mrs. S. R. Ellicott." The voice seems extremely detached.

"Oh, good morning, Mrs. Ellicott. This is Oliver—Oliver Crowe, you know. Is Nancy there?"

Nor does it appear inclined toward lengthy conversation—the voice at the other end. "No."

"Well, when will she be in? I've got to take the five o'clock train Mrs. Ellicott—I've simply got to—I may lose my job if I don't—but I've got to talk to her first—I've got to explain—"

"There can be very little good, I think, in your talking to her Mr. Crowe. She has told me that you both consider the engagement at an end."

"But that's impossible, Mrs. Ellicott—that's too absurd" Oliver felt too much as if he were fighting for life against something invisible to be careful about his words. "I know we quarrelled last night—but it was all my fault, I didn't mean anything—I was going to call her up the first thing this morning but you see, they wouldn't let me out—"

Then he stopped with a grim realization of just what it was that he had said. There was a long fateful pause from the other end of the wire.

"I'm afraid I don't quite understand, Mr. Crowe."

"They wouldn't let me out. I was—er—detained—ah—kept in."

"Detained?" The inflection is politely inquisitive.

"Yes, detained. You see—I—you—oh dammit, I was in jail." This time the pause that follows had to Oliver much of the quality of that little deadly hush that will silence all earth and sky in the moment before Last Judgment. Then—

"*In jail,*" said the voice with an accent of utter finality.

"Yes—yes—oh it wasn't anything—I could explain in five seconds if I saw her—it was all a misunderstanding—I called the policeman a boob but I didn't mean it—I don't see yet why he took offence—it was just—"

He was stifling inside the airless booth—he trickled all over. This was worse than being court-martialled. And still the voice did not speak.

"Can't you understand?" he yelled at last with more strength of lung than politeness.

"I quite understand, Mr. Crowe. You were in jail. No doubt we shall read all about it in tomorrow's papers."

"No you won't—I gave somebody else's name."

"Oh." Mrs. Ellicott was ticking off the data gathered so far on her fingers. The brutal quarrel with Nancy. The rush to the nearest blind-tiger. The debauch. The insult to Law. The drunken struggle. The prison. The alias. And now the attempt to pretend that nothing had happened—when the criminal in question was doubtless swigging from a pocket-flask at this very moment for the courage to support his flagrant impudence in trying to see Nancy again. All this passed through Mrs. Ellicott's mind like a series of colored pictures in a Prohibition *brochure*.

"But I can explain that too. I can explain everything. Please, Mrs. Ellicott—"

"Mr. Crowe, this conversation has become a very painful one. Would it not be wiser to close it?"

Oliver felt as if Mrs. Ellicott had told him to open his bag and when he did so had pointed sternly at a complete set of burglar's tools on top of his dress-shirts.

"Can-I-see-Nancy?" he ended desperately, the words all run together:

But the voice that answered was very firm with rectitude.

"Nancy has not the slightest desire to see you, Mr. Crowe. Now or ever." Mrs. Ellicott asked pardon inwardly for the lie with a false humility—if Nancy will not save herself from this young man whom she has always disliked and who has just admitted to being a jailbird in fact and a drunkard by implication, she will.

"I should think you would find it easier hearing this from me than you would from her. She has found it easier to say." "But, Mrs. Ellicott—"

"There are things that take a little too much explaining to explain, Mr. Crowe." The meaning seemed vague but the tone was doomlike enough. "And in any case" the voice ended with a note of flat triumph, "Nancy will not be home until dinnertime so you could not possibly telephone her before the departure of your train."

"Oh."

"Good-by, Mr. Crowe," and a click at the other end showed that Mrs. Ellicott had hung up the receiver, leaving him to shriek "But listen—" pitiably into the little black mouthpiece in front of him until Central cut in on him angrily with "Say, whatcha tryin' to do, fella? Break my ear?"

XXII

After cindery hours in a day coach—the fine and the loss of his Pullman reservation have left him with less than three dollars in cash—Oliver crawls into Vanamee and Company's about four in the afternoon. Everybody but Mrs. Wimple and Mr. Tickler is out of Copy for the moment and the former greets him with coy wit.

"Been taking your vacation at Newport, Crowie? Or didja sneak the Frisco account away from Brugger's Service when you were out West?"

"Oh, no, got jugged—that was all," says Oliver quite truthfully if tiredly and Mrs. Wimple crows at the jest with high laughter. Oliver marvels at the fact that everybody should seem to think it so humorous to be jailed.

"Why, Crowie, you naughty little boy! Oh mischief, mischief!" and she scrapes one index finger over the other at him in a try for errant childishness. Then she and her perfume come closer and this time she looks around before she speaks and there is some little real concern in her voice.

"Listen, Crowie—you better watch your step, boy—I'm telling you straight. Old Man Alley was real sore when you didn't blow in yesterday—it was one of Vanamee's bad days when his eye gets twitchy and he was rearing around cursing everybody out and giving an oration on office discipline that'd a made a goat go laugh itself ill. And then Alley got hold of Delier and they are both talking about you—I know because Delier said 'Oh give him another chance' and Alley said 'What's the use, Deller—he's been here eight months and he doesn't seem to really get the hang of things,' in that snippy little way and then 'I can't stand breaches of discipline like this.' You know how nervous it gets him if as much as a fastener is out of place on his desk—and Winslow's got a kid cousin he wants to put in here and if you don't act like mama's darling for a while—"

She is ready to go on indefinitely, but Oliver thanks her abstractedly—it is decent of the old girl after all—grunts "Guess I better start in looking busy now, Mrs. Wimple!" and sits down at his desk.

A note from Deller with five pencil sketches attached of the new trade figures for Brittlekin—two bloated looking children with inkblot eyes looking greedily at an enormous bar of peanut candy. "Dear Crowe: Will you give me copy on these as soon as possible—something snappy this time.—E. B. D." A memorandum, "Mr. Piper called you 4 P.M. Monday. Wishes you to call him as soon as possible." The United Steel Frame Pulley layouts and another note from Deller, "This is LATE. DO something." Back to pulleys again and the crowded sweat-box of the copy room and twenty-five dollars a week with the raise gone glimmering now—

And Nancy is lost.

Oliver sits looking at the layouts for United Steel Frame Pulleys for half-an-hour without really doing anything but sharpen and resharpen a pencil. Mrs. Wimple wonders if he's sick—he ain't white or anything but he looks just like Poppa did the time he came back and told Momma, "Momma the bank has bust and our funds has went." She watches him eagerly—gee, it'd be exciting if he fainted or did anything queer! He said he'd been in jail too—Mrs. Wimple shivers—but he's so comical you never can tell what he really means—that way he looks may be just what she saw in a movie once about "the pallid touch of the prison." If it's indigestion, though, he ought to try Pepsolax—that certainly eases you up right—

Finally Oliver stacks all the layouts together in a careful pile and goes in to see Mr. Alley. That precise and toothy little sub-deity does not seem extremely enthusiastic over his return.

"Well, Mr. Crowe, so you got back? What detained you?"

"Police" says Oliver with a faint smile and Mr. Alley laughs dutifully enough though rather in a "here, here, we must get down to business" way. Then he fusses with his pencil a little.

"I'm glad you came in, Crowe. I wanted to see you about that matter. It is not so much that we begrudge—but in a place like this where everyone must work shoulder to shoulder—and purely as a point of office discipline—Mr. Vanamee is rather rigid in regard to that and your work so far has really hardly justified—"

"Oh that's all right, Mr. Alley" breaks in Oliver, though not rudely, he is much too fagged to be rude, "I'm leaving at the end of the week if it's convenient to you."

"Well, *really*, Mr. Crowe." But in spite of his diplomatic surprise he hardly seems distressfully perturbed. "I hope it is not because you feel we have treated you unfairly—" he begins again a little anxiously—under all his feathers of fussiness he is essentially kindly.

"Oh no, I'm just leaving."

There are more diplomatic exchanges but when they have ended Oliver goes back to Copy, remarks "Quitting Saturday, Mrs. Wimple," gets his hat and goes off a quarter of an hour earlier than he ever has before, leaving the rest of Copy to match pennies and opinions till closing time on the question as to whether he fired himself or was fired.

XXIII

Jane Ellen swayed back and forth in the porch hammock, hugging herself with fat arms. All her dolls lay spread out wretchedly on the floor beneath her, she had stripped them of every rag and they had the dejected appearance of victims ready for sacrifice to Baal. "The Choolies are mad!" she sang to herself, "The Choolies are mad!"

It had been a perfectly sensible idea to try and water the flowers on the parlor carpet with her doll's watering pot— those flowers hadn't had any water for an awful long time. But Mother had punished her in the Third Degree which was by hairbrush and Aunt Elsie had taken the watering-pot away and Rosalind and Dickie had put on such offensively virtuous expressions as soon as they heard her being punished that she was mad at them all. And not ordinarily mad—not mad just by herself—the Choolies were divinely incensed as well.

"The Choolies are mad!" she hummed again like a battle-cry "Choolies are dolls and all the Choolies are mad!"

The Choolies were only mad on rare occasions. It took something genuinely out of the ordinary to turn an inoffensive pink celluloid doll with one of its legs off into an angry Choolie. But when they were mad the family had discovered by painful experience that the only thing to do was to leave Jane Ellen quite entirely alone.

"The Choolies are mad, mad, mad!" she chanted end chanted,

her plump legs swinging, her mouth set like a prophet's calling down lightnings on Babylon the splendid.

Then she stopped swinging. Somebody was coming up the path—any of the people she was mad at?—no—only Uncle Ollie. Were the Choolies mad at Uncle Ollie? She considered a moment.

"Hello, Jane Ellen, how goes it?"

The small mouth was full of rebellion.

"Um mad!"

"Oh—sorry. What about?"

Defiantly

"Um *mad*. And the Choolies are mad—they're mad—they're mad—"

Oliver looked at her a moment but was much too wise to smile.

"They aren't mad at you, but they're mad at Motha and Aunt Elsie and Ro and Dickie and oh—evvabody!" Jane Ellen stated graciously.

"Well, as long as they aren't mad at me—Any letters for me, Jane Ellen?" "Yash."

Oliver found them on the desk, looked them over, once, twice. A letter from Peter Piper. Two advertisements. A letter with a French stamp. Nothing from Nancy.

He went out on the porch again to read his letters, to the accompaniment of Jane Ellen's untirable chant. "The Choolies are mad" buzzed in his ears, "The Choolies, the Choolies are mad." For a moment he saw the Choolies; they were all women like Mrs. Ellicott but they stood up in front of him taller than the sky and one of them had hidden Nancy away in her black silk pocket—put her somewhere, where he never would see her again.

"Ollie, you look at me sternaly—*don't* look at me so sternaly, Ollie—the Choolies aren't mad at you—" said Jane Ellen anxiously. "Fy do you look at me so sternaly?"

He grinned his best at her. "Sorry, Jane Ellen. But my girl's chucked me and I've chucked my job—and consequently all *my* choolies are mad—"

XXIV

That night was distinguished by four uneasy meals in different localities. The first was Oliver's and he ate it as if he were consuming sawdust while the Crowes talked all around him in the suppressed voices of people watching a military funeral pass to its muffled drums. Mrs. Crowe was too wise to try and comfort him in public except by silence and even Dickie was still too surprised at Oliver's peevish "Oh *get* out, kid" when he tried to drag him into their usual evening boxing match to do anything but confide despondently to his mother that he doesn't see why Oliver has to act so *queer* about any girl.

The second meal was infinitely gayer on the surface though a certain kind of strainedness a little like the strainedness in the pauses of a perfectly friendly football game when both sides are too evenly matched to score ran through it. Still, whatever strainedness there was could hardly have been Mrs. Severance's fault.

The impeccable Elizabeth showed no surprise at being told she could have the day and needn't be back till breakfast tomorrow. She might have thought that there seemed to be a good deal of rather perishable food in the icebox to be wasted, if Mrs. Severance were going to have dinner out. But Elizabeth had always been one of the rare people who took pride in "knowing when they were suited" and the apartment on Riverside Drive had suited her perfectly for four years. She was also a great deal too clever to abstract any of those fragile viands to take to her widowed sister on Long Island—Mrs.

Stephen Vincent Benet

Severance is so good at finding uses for all sorts of odd things—Elizabeth felt quite sure she would find some use or other for these too.

Ted Billett certainly found a good deal of use for some of it, thought Mrs. Severance whimsically. It had hardly been a Paolo and Francesca *diner-a-deux*—both had been much too frankly hungry when they came to it and Ted's most romantic remarks so far had been devoted to a vivid appreciation of Mrs. Severance's housekeeping. But all men are very much like hungry little boys every so often, Mrs. Severance reflected.

Ted really began to wonder around nine-thirty. At first there had been only coming in and finding Rose just through setting the table and then they had been too busy with dinner and their usual fence of talk to allow for any unfortunate calculations as to how Mrs. Severance could do it on her salary. But what a perfect little apartment—and even supposing all the furniture and so forth were family inheritances, and they fitted each other much too smoothly for that, the mere upkeep of the place must run a good deal beyond any "Mode" salary. Mr. Severance? Ted wasn't sure. Oh, well he was too comfortable at the moment to look gift horses of any description too sternly in the mouth.

Rose *was* beautiful—it was Ted and Rose by now. He would like to see someone paint her sometime as Summer, drowsy and golden, passing through fields of August, holding close to her rich warm body the tall sheaves of her fruitful corn. And again the firelight crept close to him, and under its touch all his senses stirred like leaves in light wind, glad to be hurt with firelight and then left soothed and heavy and warm.

Only now he had a charm against what the firelight meant—what it had been meaning more and more these last few weeks with Rose Severance. It was not a very powerful-looking charm—a dozen lines of a letter from Elinor Piper asking him to come to Southampton, but it began "Dear Ted" and ended "Elinor" and he thought it would serve.

That ought to be enough—that small thing only magical from what you made it mean against what it really was—that wish that nobody could even nickname hope—to keep you cool against the waves of firelight that rose over you like the scent of a harvest meadow. It was, almost.

Rose had been telling him how unhappy she was all evening. Not whiningly—and not, as he remembered later, with any specific details—but in a way that made him feel as if he, as part of the world that had hurt her, were partly responsible. And to want exceedingly to help. And then the only way he could think of helping was to put himself like kindling into the firelight, and he mustn't do that. "Elinor" he said under his breath like an exorcism, but Rose was very breathing and good to look at and in the next chair.

His fingers took a long time getting his watch.

"I've *got* to go Rose, really."

"Must you? What's the time—eleven?—why heavens, I've kept you here ages, haven't I, and done nothing but moan about my troubles all the time."

"You know I liked it." Ted's voice was curiously boyishly honest in a way he hated but a way that was one of Rose's reasons why he was here with her.

"Well, come again," she said frankly. "It was fun. I loved it." "I will—Lord knows I thank you enough—after 252A Madison Avenue it was simply perfect. And Rose—"

"Well?"

"I'm awful damn sorry. I wish I could help."

He thought she was going to laugh. Instead she turned perfectly grave.

Stephen Vincent Benet

"I wish you could, Ted."

They shook hands—it seemed to Ted with a good deal of effort to do only that. Then they stood looking at each other.

There was so little between them—only a charm that nobody could say was even partly real—but somewhere in Ted's brain it said "Elinor" and he managed to shake hands again and get out of the door.

Mrs. Severance waited several minutes, listening, a faint smile curling her mouth with intentness and satisfaction. No, this time he wouldn't come back—nor next time, maybe—but there would be other times—-

Then she went into the pantry and started heating water for the dishes that she had explained reassuringly to Ted they were leaving for Elizabeth. There was no need at all of Elizabeth's knowing any more than was absolutely necessary.

XXV

Mr. Severance—the courtesy title at least is due him—seems to be a man with quite a number of costly possessions. At least here he is with another house, a dinner-table, servants, guests, another Mrs. Severance or somebody who seems to fill her place very adequately at the opposite end of the table, all as if Rose and the Riverside Drive apartment and reading Dickens aloud were only parts of a doll-house kept in one locked drawer of his desk.

The dinner is flawless, the guests importantly jeweled or stomached, depending on their sex, the other Mrs. Severance an admirable hostess—and yet in spite of it all, Mr. Severance does not seem to be enjoying himself as he should. But this may be due to a sort of minstrel give-and-take of dialogue that keeps going on between what he says for publication and what he thinks.

"Well, Frazee, I'll be ready to go into that loan matter with you inside a month," says his voice, and his mind "Frazee, you slippery old burglar, it won't be a month before you'll be spreading the news that my disappearance means suicide and that the Commercial is rotten, lock, stock and barrel."

"Yes, dear," in answer to a relayed query from the other Mrs. Severance. "The children took the small car to go to the dance." "And, Mary, if they'd ever been our children instead of your keeping them always yours, there wouldn't be that little surprise in store for you that I've arranged."

"Cigar, Winthrop?" "Better take two, my friend—they won't be as good after Mary has charge of that end of the house."

So it goes—until Mr. Severance has dined very well indeed. And yet Winthrop, chatting with Frazee, just before they go out of the door, finds it necessary to whisper to him for some reason—half a dozen words under cover of a discussion of what the Shipping Board's new move will mean to the mercantile marine. "I told you so, George. See his hands? The old boy's failing."

XXVI

The fourth meal is Nancy's and it doesn't seem very happy. When it is over and Mr. Ellicott has rustled himself away from intrusion behind the evening paper.

"Nobody—'phoned today—did they, mother?"

"No, dear." The voice is not as easy as it might be, but Nancy does not notice.

"Oh."

Nor does Nancy notice how hurriedly her mother's next question comes.

"Did you see Mrs. Winters, darling?"

"Oh yes—I saw her."

"And you're going on to New York?"

"Yes—next week, I think."

"With her. And going to stay with her?"

"I suppose so."

Mrs. Ellicott sighs relievedly.

"That's so nice."

Nancy will be safe now—as safe as if she were under an anesthetic. Mrs. Winters will take care of that. She must have a little talk with dear Isabella Winters. But that night Nancy is alone in her room—doing up her engagement ring and Oliver's letters in a wobbly package. She is not quite just, though, she keeps one letter—the first.

XXVII

Margaret Crowe, who, having just come to her seventeenth birthday in this present day and generation, felt it her official family duty to season the general conversation with an appropriate pepper of heartlessness, had really put it very well. She had said that while she didn't suppose one house party over Labor Day would more than partially rivet a broken heart, it honestly was a relief for everybody else to get Oliver out of the house for a while, and mother needn't look at her that way because she was as sorry as any of the rest of them for poor old Oliver but when people went about like walking cadavers and nearly bit you any time you mentioned anything that had to do with marriage, it was time they went somewhere else for a while and stayed there till they got over it.

And Mrs. Crowe, though dutifully rebuking her for her flippant treatment of a brother's pain, agreed with the sense of her remarks, if not with the wording. It had taken a good deal of quiet obstinacy on the part of the whole family to get Oliver to accept Peter Piper's invitation—Mrs. Crowe, who was understanding, knew at what cost—the cost of a man who has lost a hand's first appearance in company with the stump unbandaged—but anything would be better than the mopey Oliver of the last two weeks and a half, and Mrs. Crowe had been taught by a good deal of living the aseptic powers of having to go through the motions of ordinary life in front of a casual audience, even when it seemed that those motions were no longer of any account. So Oliver took clean flannels and a bitter mind to Southampton on the last day of August, and, as soon as he got off the train, was swung into a reel of consecutive amusements that, fortunately, allowed him little time to think.

When he did, it was only to wonder rather frigidly if this fellow with glasses who played tennis and danced and swam and watched and commented athletically on the Davis Cup finals, sitting between Elinor Piper and Juliet Bellamy whom he had taken to dances off and on ever since he had had his first pair of pumps, could really be he. The two people didn't feel in the least the same.

The two Mr. Crowes, he thought. "Mr. Oliver Crowe—meet Mr. Oliver Crowe." "On our right, ladies and gentlemen, we have one of the country's greatest curiosities—a young gentleman who insists upon going on existing when there is nothing at all that makes his existence useful or interesting or proud. A very realistic wax figure that will toddle, shoot a line and play almost any sort of game until you might easily believe it to be genuinely alive. Mr. Oliver Crowe."

The house-party was to last a week, except for Ted Billett who would have to go back after Labor Day—and before eight hours of it were over, Oliver was watching Ted with grandmotherly interest, a little mordant jealousy, and humor, that, at times, verged toward the hysterical. Nancy—and especially the loss of her—had made him sensitive as a skinless man to the winds and vagaries of other young people in love— and while Ted could look at and talk with Elinor Piper and think himself as safe as a turtle under its shell from the observations and discoveries of the rest of the party he could no more hide himself or his intentions from Oliver's painful scrutiny than he could have hidden the fact that he had suddenly turned bright green. So Oliver, a little with the sense of his own extreme generosity, but sincerely enough in the main, began to play kind shepherd, confidante, referee and second-between-the-rounds to Ted's as yet quite unexpressed strivings—and since most of him was only too willing to busy itself with anything but reminiscences of Nancy, be began to congratulate himself shortly that under his entirely unacknowledged guidance things really seemed to be getting along very well.

And here too his streak of ineradicable humor—that bright plaything made out of knives that is so fine to juggle with light-handedly until the hand meets it in its descent a fraction of a second too soon—came often and singularly to his aid. He could see himself in a property white beard stretching feeble hands in blessing over a kneeling and respectful Elinor and Ted. "Bless you my dear, dear children—for though my own happiness has gone with yester-year, at least I have made you—find each other—and perhaps, when you sit at evening among the happy shouts of your posterity—" but here Oliver broke off into a snort of laughter.

Of course Ted had confided nothing formally as yet—but then, thought Oliver sourly out of his own experience, he wouldn't; that was the way you always felt; and Ted had never been a person of easy confidences. The most he had done had been to take Oliver grimly aside from the dance they had gone to last night and explain in one ferocious and muffled sentence delivered half at Oliver and half at a large tree that if Hinky Selvage didn't stop dancing with Elinor that way he, Ted, would carry him unobtrusively behind a bush and force him to swallow most of his own front teeth. And again Oliver, looking back as a man might to the feverish details of a major operation, realized with cynic mirth that that was a very favorable symptom indeed. Oh everything was going along simply finely for Ted, if the poor fool only knew it. But that he would no more believe of course than you would a dentist who told you he wasn't going to hurt. People in love *were* poor fools—damn fools—unutterably lucky, unutterably perfect—fools.

Ted and Oliver must have one talk though before it all happened beyond redemption and Ted started wearing that beautiful anesthetized smile and began to concoct small kindly fatal conspiracies with Elinor and Oliver and some nice girl.

They hadn't had a real chance to talk since Oliver came back from St. Louis, and shortly—oh very shortly indeed by the way things looked—the only thing they would be able to talk about would be Elinor and how wonderful she and requited love and young happy marriage were—and however glad Oliver might be for Ted and his luck—he really wouldn't be able to stand that, under the present circumstances, for very long at a time. Ted would be gone into fortune—into a fortune that Oliver would have to be the last person on earth to grudge him—but that meant the end of eight years of fighting mockery and friendship together as surely as if those years were marbles and Elinor were dropping them down a well. They could pick it up later—after Ted had been married a year say—but it would have changed then, it wouldn't be the same.

Oliver smiled rather wryly. He wondered if that was at all like what Ted might have thought when he and Nancy—But that wasn't comparable in the least. But Nancy and he were different. *Nancy*—and with that, the pain came so dazzlingly for a minute that Oliver had to shut his eyes to bear it—and something that wasn't just stupidly rude had to be said to Juliet Bellamy in answer to her loud clear question as to whether he was falling asleep.

All up to and through Labor Day Oliver bluffed and manoeuvered like the head of a small but vicious Balkan State in an International Congress for Ted and Elinor, and towards tea-time, decided sardonically that it was quite time his adopted infants took any further responsibilities off his shoulders. There was no use delaying conclusions any longer— Oliver felt as he looked at his victims like a workmanlike god who simply must finish the rough draft of the particular world he is fussing with before sunset, in spite of all rebellious or slipshod qualities in its clay. There would be a dance that evening. There would be, Oliver thought with some proprietary pride, a large sentimental moon. A few craftily casual words with Elinor before dinner—a real talk with Ted in one of the intermissions of the dance—a watchdog efficiency in guarding the two from intrusion while they got the business over with neatly in any one of several very suitable spots that Oliver had picked out already in his mind's eye. And then, having thoroughly settled Ted for the rest of his years in such a solid and satisfactory way—perhaps the queer gods that had everyone in charge, in spite of their fatal leaning toward practical-joking where the literary were concerned, might find enough applause in their little tin hearts for Oliver's acquired and vicarious merit to give him in some strange and painful way another chance to be alive again and not merely the present wandering spectre-of-body that people who knew nothing about it seemed to take so unreasonably for Oliver Crowe.

So he laid his snares, feeling quite like Nimrod the mighty, though outwardly he was only kneeling on the Piper porch, waiting for the dice to come around to him in a vociferous game of crap that Juliet had organized—he seldom shot without winning now he noticed with superstitious awe. And tea passed to a sound of muffled crumpets, and everyone went up to dress for dinner.

XXVIII

Mrs. Winters' little apartment on West 79th Street—she heads letters from it playfully "The Hen Coop" for there is almost always some member of her own sex doing time with the generous Mrs. Winters. Mrs. Winters is quite celebrated in St. Louis for her personally-conducted tours of New York with stout Middle-Western matrons or spectacled school girls east for visits and clothes—Mrs. Winters has the perfectly-varnished manners, the lust for retailing unimportant statistics and the supercilious fixed smile of a professional guide. Mrs. Winters' little apartment, that all the friends who come to her to be fed and bedded and patronized tell her is so charmingly New Yorky because of her dear little kitchenette with the asthmatic gas-plates, the imitation English plate-rail around the dining- room wall, the bookcase with real books—a countable number of them—and on top of it the genuine signed photograph of Caruso for which Mrs. Winters paid the sum she always makes you guess about, at a charity-bazaar.

Mrs. Winters herself—the Mrs. Winters who is *so* interested in young people as long as they will do exactly what she wants them to—every inch of her from her waved white hair to the black jet spangles on her dinner gown or the notes of her "cultivated" voice as frosted and glittery and artificial as a piece of *glace* fruit. And with her, Nancy, dressed for dinner too, because Mrs. Winters feels it to be one's duty to oneself to dress for dinner always, no matter how much one's guests may wish to relax—Nancy as much out of place in the apartment whose very cushions seem to smell of that modern old-maidishness that takes itself for superior feminist virtue as a crocus would be in an exhibition of wool flowers—a Nancy who doesn't talk much and has faint blue stains under her eyes.

"So everything went very satisfactorily indeed today, dear Nancy?"

Mrs. Winters' voice implies the uselessness of the question. Nancy is staying with Mrs. Winters—it would be very strange indeed if even the least important accompaniments of such a visit were not of the most satisfactory kind.

"Yes, Mrs. Winters. Nothing particularly happened, that is—but they like my work."

"Yes, dear," Mrs. Winters croons at her, she is being motherly. The effect produced is rather that of a sudden assumption of life and vicarious motherhood on the part of a small, brightly-painted porcelain hen.

"Then they will be sending you over shortly, no doubt? Across the wide wide sea—" adds Mrs. Winters archly, but Nancy is too tired-looking to respond to the fancy.

"I suppose they will when they get ready," she answers briefly and returns to her chicken-croquette with the thought that in its sleekness, genteelness, crumblingness, and generally unnourishing qualities it is really rather like Mrs. Winters. An immense desire, after two weeks of Mrs. Winters' mental and physical cuisine for something as hearty and gross as the mere sight of a double planked steak possesses her achingly—but Mrs. Winters was told once that she "ate like a bird."

"Well, in that case, dear Nancy, you certainly must not leave New York indefinitely without making the most of your opportunities," Mrs. Winters' tones are full of genteel decision. "I have made out a little list, dear Nancy, of some things which I thought, in my funny old way, might possibly be worth your while. We will talk it over after dinner, if you like—"

"Thank you so much, dear Mrs. Winters" says Nancy with dutiful hopelessness. She is only too well acquainted with Mrs. Winters' little lists. "As an *artist*, as an *artist*, dear Nancy, especially." Mrs. Winters breathes somewhat heavily, "Things That Should Interest you. Nothing Bizarre, you understand, Nothing Merely Freakish—but some of the Things in New York that I, Personally, have found Worth While."

The Things that Mrs. Winters Has Found Personally Worth While include a great many public monuments. She will give Nancy a similar list of Things Worth While in Paris, too, before Nancy sails—and Nancy smiles acceptably as each one of them is mentioned.

Only Mrs. Winters cannot see what Nancy is thinking—for if she did she might become startlingly human at once as even the most perfectly poised of spinsters is apt to do when she finds a rat in the middle of her neat white bed. For Nancy is thinking quite freely of various quaint and everlasting places of torment that might very well be devised for Mrs. Winters— and of the naked fact that once arrived in Paris it will matter very little to anybody what becomes of her and least of all to herself—and that Mrs. Winters doesn't know that she saw a chance mention of Mr. Oliver Crowe, the author of "Dancer's Holiday" today in the "Bookman" and that she cut it out because it had Oliver's name in it and that it is now in the smallest pocket of her bag with his creased and recreased first letter and the lucky piece she had from her nicest uncle and a little dim photograph of Mr. Ellicott and half a dozen other small precious things.

XXIX

The dance is at the Piper's this time—the last Piper dance of the Southampton season and the biggest—other people may give dances after it but everybody who knows will only think of them as relatively pleasant or useless addenda. The last Piper Dance has been the official period to the Southampton summer ever since Elinor's *debut*—and this time the period is sure to be bigger and rounder than ever since it closes the most successful season Southampton has ever had.

Nothing very original about its being a masquerade, from Mr. Piper a courteously grey-haired mandarin in jade-green robes beside Mrs. Piper—lovely Mary Embree that was—in the silks of a Chinese empress, heavy and shining and crusted as the wings of a jeweler's butterfly, her reticent eyes watching the bright broken patterns of the dancing as impassively as if she were viewing men being tortured or invested with honor from the Dragon Throne, to Oliver, a diffident Pierrot who has discovered no even bearably comfortable way of combining spectacles and a mask, and Peter who is gradually turning purple under the furs of a dancing bear. Nothing much out of the ordinary in the tunes and the three orchestras and the fact that a dozen gentlemen dressed as the Devil are finding their tails very inconvenient as regards the shimmy and a dozen Joans of Arc are eying each other with looks of dumb hatred whenever they pass. Nothing singular about the light-heart throb of the music, the smell of powder and scent and heat and flowers, the whole loose drifting garland of the dancers, blowing over and around the floor in the idle designs of sand,

Stephen Vincent Benet

floating like scraps of colored paper through a smooth wind heavy with music as the hours run away like light water through the fingers. But outside the house the Italian gardens are open, little lanterns spot them like elf-lights, shining on hedge-green, pale marble; the night is pallid with near and crowded stars, the air warm as Summer water, sweet as dear youth.

The unmasking is to take place at midnight and it is past eleven when Oliver drops back into the stag line after being stuck for a dance and a half with a leaden-footed human flower-basket who devoted the entire time to nervous giggles and the single coy statement that she just knew he never could guess who she was but she recognized him perfectly. He starts looking around for Ted. There he is, scanning the clown's parade with the eyes of an anxious hawk, disgruntled nervousness plain in every line of his body. Then Oliver remembers that he saw a slim Chinese girl in loose blue silks go off the floor ten minutes or so ago with a tall musketeer. He goes over and touches Ted on a particolored arm—the latter is dressed as a red and gilt harlequin—and feels the muscles he touches twitch under his hand.

"Cigarette? It's getting hotter than cotton in here—they'll have to open more windows—"

"What?" Then recognizing voice and glasses "Oh yeah—guess so—awful mob, isn't it?" and they thread their way out into the cool.

They wander down from the porch and into the gardens, past benches where the talk that is going on seems to be chiefly in throaty undertones and halts nervously as their steps crunch past.

"The beautiful and damned!" says Oliver amusedly, then a little louder *"Amusez vous bien, mes enfants"* at a small and carefully modulated shriek that comes from the other side of the low hedge, "The night's still young. But Good Lord, isn't there *any* place in the whole works where two respectable people can sit without feeling like chaperones?"

They find one finally—it is at the far end of the gardens—a seat the only reason for whose obvious desertion seems to be, comments Oliver, that some untactful person has strung a dim but still visible lantern directly above it—and relapses upon it silently. It is not until the first cigarettes of both are little red dying stars on the grass beside them that either really starts to talk.

"Cool," says Oliver, stretching his arms. The night lies over them light as spray—a great swimming bath and quietness of soft black, hushed silver—above them the whole radiant helmet of heaven is white with its stars. From the house they have left, glowing yellow in all its windows, unreal against the night as if it were only a huge flat toy made out of paper with a candle burning behind it, comes music, blurred but insistent, faint as if heard over water, dull and throbbing like horse-hoofs muffled with leather treading a lonely road.

"Um. Good party."

"Real Piper party, Ted. And, speaking of Pipers, friend Peter certainly seems to be enjoying himself—"

"Really?"

"Third bench on the left as we came down. Never go to a costume-party dressed as a dancing-bear if you want to get any quiet work in on the side. Rule One of Crowe's Social Code for Our Own First Families."

Ted chuckles uneasily and there is silence for another while as they smoke. Both are in very real need of talking to each other but must feel their way a little carefully because they are friends. Then—

"I," says Ted and—

"You," says Oliver, simultaneously. Both laugh and the little tension that has grown up between them snaps at once.

"I suppose you know that Nancy's and my engagement went bust about three weeks ago," begins Oliver with elaborate calm, his eyes fixed on his shoes.

Ted clears his throat.

"Didn't *know*. Afraid it was something like that though—way you were looking," he says, putting his words one after the other, as slowly as if he were building with children's blocks. "What was it?" Don't tell me unless you want to, of course— *you* know—-"

"Want to, rather." Ted knows that he is smiling, and how, though he is not looking at his face. "After all—old friends, all that. My dear old College chum," but the mockery breaks down. "My fault, I guess," he says in a voice like metal.

"It was, Ted. Acted like a fool. And then, this waiting business—not much use going over that, now. But it's broken. Got my—property—such as it was all back in a neat little parcel two weeks ago. That's why I quit friend Vanamee—you ought to have known from that."

"Did, I suppose, only I hoped it wasn't. I'm damn sorry, Ollie.

"Thanks, Ted."

They shake hands, but not theatrically.

"Oh well—oh hell—oh dammit, you know how blasted sorry I am. That's all I can say, I guess—"

"Well, so am I. And it was my fault, chiefly. And that's all I can say."

"Look here, though." Ted's voice is doing its best to be logical in spite of the fact that two things, the fact that he is unutterably sorry for Oliver and the fact that he mustn't show it in silly ways, are fighting in him like wrestlers. "Are you sure it's as bad as all that? I mean girls——" Ted flounders hopelessly between his eagerness to help and his knowledge that it will take ungodly tact. "I mean, Nancy's different all right—but they change their minds—and they come around—and—"

Oliver spreads out his hands. It is somehow queerly comforting not to let himself be comforted in any degree. "What's the use? Tried to explain—got her mother—Nancy was out but she certainly left a message—easier if we never saw each other again—well—Then she sent back everything—she knew I'd tried to phone her—tried to explain—never a word since then except my name and address on the package—oh it's over, Ted. Feenee. But it's pretty well smashed me. For the present, at least."

"But if you started it," Ted says stubbornly.

"Oh I did, of course—gentlemanly supposition anyhow—that's why—don't you see?"

"Can't say I do exactly."

"Well?"

"Well?"

"We're both of us too proud, Ted. And too poor. And starting again—can't you—visualize—it wouldn't be the way it was—only both of us thinking about *that* all the time—and *still* we couldn't get married. I've got less right than ever, now—oh, but how *could* we after what we've said—" and this time his voice has lost all the attitudes of youth, it is singularly older and seems to come from the center of a place full of pain.

"I wish I could help, though, Ollie. You know," says Ted.

"Wish you could." Then later, "Thanks." "Welcome."

Both smoke and are silent for a time, remembering small things out of the last eight years.

"But what are you going to do, Ollie, now you've kissed the great god Advertising a fond good-by?"

Ollie stirs uneasily.

"Dunno—exactly. I told you about those two short stories Easten wanted me to take out of my novel? Well, I've done it and sent 'em in—and he'll buy 'em all right."

"That's fine!"

"It's a little money, anyhow. And then—remember Dick Lamoureux?"

"Yes."

"Got a letter from him right after—I came back from St. Louis. Well, he's got a big job with the American Express in Paris—European Advertising Manager or something like that—he's been crazy to have either of us come over ever since that idea of the three of us getting an apartment on the *Rive Gauche* fell through. Well, he says, if I can come over, he'll get me some sort of a job—not much to go on at first but they want people who are willing to stay—enough to live on anyway—I want to get out of the country, Ted."

"Should think you would. Good Lord—Paris! Why you lucky, lucky Indian!" says Ted affectionately. "When'll you leave?" "Don't know. He said cable him if I really decided—think I will. They need men and I can get a fair enough letter from Vanamee. I've been thinking it over ever since the letter came—wondering if I'd take it. Think I will now. Well."

"Well, I wish I was going along, Crowe."

And this time Oliver is really able to smile.

"No, you don't."

"Oh well—but, honestly—well, no, I suppose I don't. And I suppose *that's* something you know all about, too, you—private detective!"

"Private detective! Why, you poor ass, if you haven't noticed how I've been playing godmother to you all the way through this house-party—"

"I have. I suppose I'd thank anybody else. Coming from you, though, I can only say that such was both my hope and my expectation."

"Oh, you *perfect* ass!" Both laugh, a little unsteadily.

"Well, Ollie, what think?" says Ted, finding some difficulty with his words for some reason or other.

"Think? Can't tell, my amorous child. Coldly considered, I think you've got a good show—and I'm very strong for it, needless to say—and if you don't go and put it over pretty soon I'll be intensely annoyed—one of the pleasures I've promised myself for years and years has been getting most disgracefully fried at your wedding, Ted."

"Well, tonight is going to be zero hour, I think." Ted proceeds with a try at being flippant and Oliver cackles with mirth.

"I knew it. I knew it. Old Uncle Ollie, the Young Proposer's Guide and Pocket Companion." Then his voice changes. "Luck," he says briefly.

"Thanks. Need it."

"Of course I'm not worthy," Ted begins diffidently but Oliver stops him.

"They never are. I wasn't. But that doesn't make any difference. You've got to—*n'est-ce pas?*"

"You old bum! Yes. But when I think of it——"

"Don't"

"But leaving out everything else—it seems so damned *cheeky!* When Elinor's got everything, including all the money in the world, and I—"

"We talked that over a long time ago, remember? And remember what we decided—that it didn't matter, in this year and world at least. Of course I'm assuming that you're really in love with her—"

"I am," from Ted very soberly. "Oh I am, all right."

"Well then, go ahead. And, Theodore, I shall watch your antic motions with the greatest sarcastic delight, both now and in the future—either way it breaks. Moreover I'll take anybody out of the action that you don't want around—and if there were anything else I could do—"

"Got to win off my own service," says Ted. "You know. But thanks all the same. Only when I think of—some incidents of Paris—and how awful near I've come to making a complete fool of myself with that Severance woman in the last month—well—"

"Look here, Ted." Oliver is really worried. "You're not going to let that—interfere—are you? Right now?"

"I've got to tell her." Ted's smile is a trifle painful. "Got to, you know. Oh not that. But France. The whole business."

"But good heavens, man, you aren't going to make it the start of the conversation?"

"Well—maybe not. But it's all got to be—explained. Only way I'll ever feel decent—and I don't suppose I'll feel too decent then."

"But Ted—oh it's your game, of course. Only I don't think it's being—fair—to either of you to tell her just now."

"Can't help it, Ollie." Ted's face sets into what Oliver once christened his "mule-look." "I've thought it over backwards and sideways and all around the block—and I can't squirm out of it because it'll be incredibly hard to do. As a matter of fact," he pauses, "it'll tell itself, you know, probably," he ends, more prophetically than he would probably care to know.

"Well, I simply *don't* see—"

"*Must*," and after that Oliver knows there is very little good of arguing the point much further. He has known Ted for eight years without finding out that a certain bitter and Calvinistic penchant for self-crucifixion is one of his ruling forces—and one of those least easily deduced from his externals. Still he makes a last effort.

"Now don't start getting all tied up about that. Keep your mind on Elinor."

"That's not—hard."

"Good—I see that you have all the proper reactions. And you'll excuse me for saying that *I* don't think she's too good for you—and even if she were she'd have to marry somebody, you know—and when you put it, put it straight, and let Paris and everything else you're worrying about go plumb to hell! And that's good advice."

"I know it. I'll tell you of course."

"Well, I should *think* you would!"

Oliver looks at his watch. "Great Scott—they'll be unmasking in twenty minutes. And I've got to go back and cut Juliet out of the herd and take her to supper—"

They rise and look at each other. Then

"Hope this is the last time, Ted, old fel—which isn't any reflection on the last eight years odd," says Oliver slowly, and their hands grip once and hard. Then they both start talking fast as they walk back to the house to cover the unworthy emotion. But just as they are going in the door, Oliver hisses into Ted's ear, an advisory whisper,

"Now go and eat all the supper you can, you idiot—it always helps."

XXX

The parti-colored harlequin and the young Chinese lady in blue silks are walking the Italian gardens, talking about nothing in particular. Ted has managed to discuss the moon— it is high now, a round white lustre—the night, which is warm—the art of garden decoration, French, English and Italian—the pleasantness of Southampton after New York—all with great nervous fluency but so completely as if he had met Elinor for the first time ten minutes ago that she is beginning to wonder why, if he dislikes her as much as that, he ever suggested leaving the dance-floor at all.

Ted, meanwhile, is frantically conscious of the fact that they have reached the end of the garden, are turning back, and still he is so cripplingly tongue-tied about the only thing he really wishes to say that he cannot even get the words out to suggest their sitting down. It is not until he stumbles over a pebble while passing a small hard marble seat set back in a nest of hedge that he manages to make his first useful remark of the promenade.

"Ah—a bench!" he says brightly, and then, because that sounded so completely imbecile, plunges on.

"Don't you want to sit down a minute, Elinor?—I—you—it's so cool—so warm, I mean—" He closes his mouth firmly— what a *ghastly* way to begin!

But Elinor says "Yes" politely and they try to adapt themselves

Stephen Vincent Benet

to the backless ornamental bench, Ted nervously crossing and recrossing his legs until he happens to think that Elinor certainly never would marry anybody with St. Vitus' Dance.

"Can't tell you how nice it's been this time, Elinor. And you've been—" There, things are going better—at least, he has recovered his voice.

"Why, you know how much we love to have you, Ted," says Elinor and Ted feels himself turn hot and cold as he was certain you never really did except in diseases. But then she adds, "You and Ollie and Bob Templar, and, oh, all Peter's friends."

He looks at her steadily for a long moment—the blue silks of her costume suit her completely. She is there, black hair and clear eyes, small hands and mouth pure as the body of a dream and elvish with thoughts like a pansy—all the body of her, all that people call her. And she is so delicately removed from him—so clean in all things where he is not—that he knows savagely within him that there can be no real justice in a world where he can even touch her lightly, and yet he must touch her because if he does not he will die. All the things he meant to say shake from him like scraps of confetti, he does not worry any more about money or seeming ridiculous or being worthy, all he knows at all in the world is his absolute need of her, a need complete as a child's and so choosing any words that come.

"Listen—do you like me?" says the particolored harlequin and all the sharp leaves of the hedge begin to titter as wind runs over them at one of the oldest and least sensible questions in the world.

The young Chinese lady turns toward the harlequin. There is some laughter in her voice and a great deal of surprise.

"Why, Ted, of course—why, why shouldn't I?—You're Peter's friend and—"

"Oh, I don't mean *that*!" The harlequin's hands twist at each other till the knuckles hurt, but he seems to have recovered most voluble if chaotic powers of speech.

"That was silly, asking that—but it's hard—when you care for anybody so much you can't *see*—when you love them till they're the only thing there *is* you care about—and you know you're not fit to touch them—not worthy of them—that they're thousands of times too good for you but—oh, Elinor, Elinor, I just can't stand it any more! Do you love me, Elinor, because I love you as I never loved anything else in the world?"

The young Chinese lady doesn't seem to be quite certain of just what is happening. She has started to speak three times and stopped each time while the harlequin has been waiting with the suspense of a man hanging from Heaven on a pack-thread. But then she does speak.

"I think I do, Ted—oh, Ted, I know I do," she says uncertainly—and then Oliver, if he were there, would have stepped forward to bow like an elegant jack-knife at the applause most righteously due him for perfect staging, for he really could not have managed better about the kiss that follows if he had spent days and days showing the principals how to rehearse it.

And then something happens that is as sudden as a bubble's going to pieces and most completely out of keeping with any of Oliver's ideas on how love should be set for the theatre. For "Oh, what am I *doing*?" says the harlequin in the voice of a man who has met his airy double alone in a wood full of ghosts and seen his own death in its face, and he crumples into a loose bag of parti-colored silks, his head in his hands. [Illustration: The Young Chinese Lady is Shrinking Inside Her Silks] It would be nothing very much to any sensible person, no doubt—the picture that made itself out of cold dishonorable fog in the instant of peace after their double release from pain. It was only the way that Elinor looked at him after the kiss—and remembering the last time he saw his own diminished

Stephen Vincent Benet

little image in the open eyes of a girl.

The young Chinese lady is shrinking inside her silks as if frost had touched her—all she knows is that she doesn't understand. And then there is the harlequin looking at her with his face gone suddenly pinched and odd as if he had started to torture himself with his own hands; and the fact that he will not touch her, and what he says.

"Oh, Elinor, darling. Oh, I can't tell you, I can't."

"But what *is* it, Ted?"

"It's this—it's what I meant to tell you before I ever told you I loved you—what I haven't any right not to tell you—and I guess that the fact I didn't, shows pretty well what sort of a fellow I am. Do you really think you know about me, dear— do you really think you do?"

"Why, of course, Ted." The voice is still a little chill with the fright he gave her, but under that it is beautifully secure.

"Well, you don't. And, oh Lord, why couldn't it have happened before I went to France!—because then it would have been all different and I'd have had some sort of a right— not a right, maybe—but anyhow, I could have come to you— straight. I can't now, dear, that's all."

The voice halts as if something were breaking to pieces inside of it.

"I can't bring you what you'd bring me. Oh, it isn't any-thing—physically—dangerous—that way—I—was—lucky." The words space themselves as slowly as if each one of them burnt like acid as it came. "It's—just—that. Just that—while I was in France—I went over—all the hurdles—and then a few more, I guess—and I've got to—tell you about it—because I love you—and because I wouldn't dare love you, even—if I didn't—tell you the truth. You see. But, oh my God, I never thought it would—hurt so!" and the parti-colored body of the harlequin is shaken with a painful passion that seems ridiculously out of keeping with his motley. But all that the young Chinese lady feels is that for a single and brittle instant she and somebody else had a star in their hands that covered them with light clean silver, and that now the conjuror who made the star out of nothing and gave it to her is showing her just why there never was any star. Moreover, she has only known she was in love for the last five minutes—and that is hardly long enough for her to discover that love itself is too living to be very much like any nice girl's dreams of it—and the shock of what Ted has said has brought every one of her mother's reticent acid hints on the general uncleanliness of Man too prickling-close to her mind. And she can't understand—she never will understand, she thinks with dull pain.

"Oh how *could* you, Ted? How *could* you?" she says as he waits as a man walking the plank might wait for the final gentle push that will send him overboard.

"Oh, I know it was fine of you to tell me—but it's just spoiled everything forever. Oh, Ted, how *could* you?" and then she is half-running, half-walking, up the path toward the porch and all she knows is that she must get somewhere where she can be by herself. The harlequin does not follow her.

Stephen Vincent Benet

XXXI

Oliver, in the middle of a painfully vivid dream in which he has just received in the lounge of a Yale Club crowded with whispering, pointing spectators the news that Miss Nancy Ellicott of St. Louis has eloped with the Prince of Wales, wakes, to hear someone stumbling around the room in the dark.

"That you, Ted?"

"Yes. Go to bed."

"Can't—I'm there. What's time?"

"'Bout five, I guess." Ted doesn't seem to want to be very communicative.

"Um." A pause while Oliver remembers what it was he wanted to ask Ted about and Ted undresses silently.

"Well—congratulations?"

Ted's voice is very even, very controlled.

"Sorry, Ollie. Not even with all your good advice."

"*Honestly?*"

"Uh-huh." "Well, look here—better luck next time, anyway.

It's all—"

"It's all over, Ollie. I'm getting out of here tomorrow before most of them are up. Special breakfast and everything—called back to town by urgent legal affairs." He laughs, rather too barkingly for Oliver to like it.

"Oh, Hell!"

"Correct."

"Well, she's—"

"She's an angel, Ollie. But I had to tell her—about France. That broke it. D'you wonder?"

"Oh, you poor, damn, honorable, simple-minded, blessed, blasted fool! *Before* you'd really begun?"

Ted hesitates. "Y-yes."

"Oh, hell!"

"Well, if all you can do is to lie back in bed there and call on your Redeemer when—-Sorry, Ollie. But I'm not feeling too pleasant tonight."

"Well, I ought to know—"

"Forgot. You ought. Well—you do."

"But I don't see anything yet that—"

"She does."

"But—"

"Oh, Ollie, what's the use? We can both of us play Job's comforter to the other because we're pretty good friends. But you can see how my telling her would—oh well there isn't much percentage in hashing it over. I've done what I've done. If I'd known I'd have to pay for it this way, I wouldn't have—but there, we're all made like that. There's one thing I can't do—and that is get away with a thing like that on false pretences—I'd rather shoot the works on one roll and crap than use the sort of dice that behave. I went into the thing with my eyes open—now I've got to pay for it—well, what of it? It wouldn't make all the difference to a lot of girls, perhaps—a lot of the best—but it does to Elinor and she's the only person I want. If I can't have her, I don't want anything—but if I've made what all the Y.M.C.A. Christians that ever sold nickel bars of chocolate for a quarter would call a swine out of myself—well, I'm going to be a first-class swine. So put on my glad rags, Josie, I'm going to Rector's and hell!"

All this has been light enough toward the end but the lightness is not far from a very real desperation, all the same.

"Meaning by which?" Oliver queries uneasily.

"Meaning by which that some of my address for the next two-three weeks will be care of Mrs. Rose Severance, 4th floor, the Nineveh, Riverside Drive, New York—you know the place, I showed it to you once from a bus-top when we were talking the mysterious lady over. And that I don't think Mr. Theodore Billett will graduate *cum laude* from Columbia Law School. In fact, I think it very possible that Mr. Billett will join Mr. Oliver Crowe, the celebrated unpublished novelist on a pilgrimage to Paris for to cure their broken hearts and go to the devil like gentlemen. Eh, Ollie?"

"Well, that's all right for *me*," says Oliver combatively. "And I always imagined we'd find each other in hell. I'm not trying to be inhospitable with my own pet red-hot gridiron, but all the same—"

"Now, Crowe, for Pete's sake, it's five o'clock in the morning and I'm catching the 7.12—"

And Oliver is too sleepy to argue the point. Besides he knows quite well that any arguments he can use will only drive Ted, in his present state of mind, a good deal farther and faster along the road he has so dramatically picked out for himself. So, between trying to think of some means of putting either sense or the fear of God into Elinor Piper, whatever Ted may say about it, and wondering how the latter would take a suggestion to come over to Melgrove for a while instead of starting an immoral existence with that beautiful but possessive friend of Louise's, he drops off to sleep.

Stephen Vincent Benet

XXXII

Oliver had depended on Ted's noisy habits in dressing and packing to wake him and give them a chance to talk before Ted left—but when he woke it was to hear a respectful servantly voice saying "Ten o'clock, sir!" and his first look around the room showed him that Ted's bed was empty and Ted's things were gone. There was a scribbled note propped up against the mirror, though.

"Dear Ollie:

"So long—and thanks for both good advice and sympathy. The latter helped if the former didn't. Drop me a message at 252A as soon as you decide on this French proposition. I'm serious about it. TED."

By the time he had read this through, Oliver began to feel rather genuinely alarmed.

He could not believe that the whole affair between Ted and Elinor Piper had gone so utterly wrong as the note implied— he had had a whimsical superstition that it must succeed because he was playing property man to it after his own appearance as Romeo had failed—but he knew Ted and the two years' fight against the struggling nervous restlessness and discontent with everything that didn't have either speed or danger in it that the latter, like so many in his position, had had to make. His mouth tightened—no girl on earth, even Nancy, could realize exactly what that meant—the battle to recover steadiness and temperance and sanity in a temperament that was in spite of its poised externals most brilliantly sensitive, most leapingly responsive to all strong stimuli—a temperament moreover that the war and the armistice between them had turned wholly toward the stimuli of fever—and Ted had made it with neither bravado nor bluster and without any particular sense of doing very much—and now this girl was going to smash it and him together as if she were doing nothing more important than playing with jackstones.

He remembered a crowd of them talking over suicide one snowy night up in Coblenz—young talk enough but Ted had been the only one who really meant it—he had got quite vehement on picking up your proper cue for exit when you knew that your part was through or you were tired of the part. He remembered cafe hangers-on in Paris—college men—men who could talk or write or teach or do any one of a dozen things—but men who had crumbled with intention or without it under the strain of the war and the snatches of easy living to excess, and now had about them in everything they said or wore a faint air of mildew; men who stayed in Paris on small useless jobs while their linen and their language verged more and more toward the soiled second-hand—who were always meaning to go home but never went. If Ted went to Paris—with his present mind. Why Ted was his best friend, Oliver realized with a little queer shock in his mind—it was something they had never just happened to say that way. And therefore. Far be it from Oliver to be rude to the daughter of his hostess, but some things were going to be explained to Miss Elinor Piper if they had to be explained by a public spanking in the middle of the Jacobean front hall.

But then there was breakfast, at which few girls appeared, and Elinor was not one of the few. And then Peter insisted on going for a swim before lunch—and then lunch with Elinor at the other end of the table and Juliet Bellamy talking like a mechanical piano into Oliver's ear so that he had to crane his neck to see Elinor at all. What he saw, however, reassured him a little—for he had always thought Elinor one of the calmest young persons in the world, and calm young persons do not generally keep adding spoonfuls of salt abstractedly to their clam-broth till the mixture tastes like the bottom of the sea.

But even at that it was not till just before tea-time that Oliver managed to cut her away from the vociferous rest of the house-party that seemed bent on surrounding them both with the noise and publicity of a private Coney Island. Peter has expressed a fond desire to motor over to a little tea-room he knows where you can dance and the others had received the suggestion with frantic applause. Oliver was just starting downstairs after changing his shoes, cursing house-party manners in general and Juliet Bellamy in particular all over his mind when Elinor's voice came up to him from below.

"No, really, Petey. No, I know it's rude of me but honestly I am *tired* and if I'm going to feel like anything but limp *tulle* this evening. No, I'm *perfectly* all right, I just want to rest for a little while and I promise I'll be positively incandescent at dinner. No, Juliet dear, I wouldn't keep you or anybody else away from Peter's nefarious projects for the world—"

That was quite enough for Oliver—he tiptoed back and hid in his own closet—wondering mildly how he was going to explain his presence there if a search party opened the door. He heard a chorus of voices calling him from below, first warningly, then impatiently—heard Peter bounce up the stairs and yell "Ollie! Ollie, you slacker!" into his own room—and then finally the last motor slurred away and he was able to creep out of his shell.

He met Elinor on the stairs—looking encouragingly droopy, he thought.

"Why Ollie, what's the matter? The pack was howling for you all over the house—they've all gone over to the Sharley—look, I'll get you a car—" She went down a couple of steps toward the telephone.

Oliver immediately and without much difficulty put on his best expression of blight.

"Sorry, El—must have dropped off to sleep," he said unblushingly. "Lay down on my bed to sort of think some things over—and that's what happens of course. But don't bother—"

"It's no trouble. I could take you over myself but I was so sort of fagged out—that's why I didn't go with them," she added— a little uncertainly he noticed.

"And—oh it's just being silly and tired I suppose, but all of them together—"

"I know," said Oliver and hoped his voice had sounded appropriately bitter. "No reflections on you or Peter, El, you both understand and you've both been too nice for words— but some of the others sometimes—"

"Oh I'm *sorry*," said Elinor contritely, and Oliver felt somewhat as if he were swindling her out of sympathy she probably needed for herself by deliberately calling attention to his own cut finger. But it had to be done—there wasn't any sense in both of them, he and Ted, walking crippled when one of them might be able to doctor the other up by just giving up a little pride. He went on.

"So I thought—I'd just stay around here with a book or something—get some tea from your mother, later, if she were here—"

"Why, I can do that much for you, Ollie, anyway. Let's have it now."

"But look here, if you were going to do anything—" knowing that after that she could hardly say so, even if she were.

"Oh no. And besides, with both of us here and both of us blue it would be silly if we went and were melancholy at each other from opposite sides of the house." She tried to be enthusiastic. "And there's strawberry jam and muffins somewhere—the kind that Peter makes himself such a pig about—"

"Well, Elinor, you certainly are a friend—"

A little later, in a quiet corner of the porch with the tea-steam floating pleasantly from the silver nose of its pot and a decorous scarlet and yellow still-life of muffins and jam between them, Oliver felt that so far things had slid along as well as could be expected. Elinor's manners in the first place and her genuine liking for him in the second had come to his help as he knew they would—she was too concerned now with trying to comfort him in small unobtrusive ways to be on her guard herself about her own troubles. All he had to do, he knew, was to sit there and look ostentatiously brokenhearted to have the conversation move in just the directions he wished and that, though it made him feel shameless was not exactly difficult—all he required was a single thought of the last three weeks to make his acting sour perfection itself. "Greater love hath no man than this," he thought with a grotesque humor— he wondered if any of the celebrated story-book patterns of friendship from Damon and Jonathan on would have found things quite so easy if they had had to take not their lives but most of their most secret and painful inwards and put them down on a tea-table like a new species of currant bun under the eyes of a friendly acquaintance to help their real friends.

"I can't tell you how awfully decent it was of you and Peter," he began finally after regarding a buttered muffin for several minutes as if it were part of the funeral decorations for dead young love. "Asking me out here, just now. Oh I'll write you a charming bread-and-butter letter of course—but I wanted to tell you really—" He stopped and let the sentence hang with malice aforethought. Elinor's move. Trust Elinor. And the trust was justified for she answered as he wanted her to, and at once.

"Why Ollie, as if it was anything—when we've all of us more or less grown up together, haven't we—and you and Peter—" She stopped—oh what was the use of being tactful! "I suppose it sounds—put on—and—sentimental and all that—saying it," she laughed nervously, "but we—all of us—Peter and myself—we're so really *sorry*—if you'll believe us—only it was hard to know if you wanted to have us say so—how awfully sorry we were. And then asking you out here with this howling mob doesn't seem much like it, does it? but Peter was going to be here—and Ted—and I knew what friends you'd been in college—I thought maybe—but I just didn't want you to think it was because we didn't care—"

"I know—and—and—thanks—and I do appreciate, Elinor." Oliver noticed with some slight terror that his own voice seemed to be getting a little out of control. But what she had just said took away his last doubt as to whether she was really the kind of person Ted ought to marry—and in spite of feeling as if he were trapping her into a surgical operation she knew nothing about, he kept on.

"It gets pretty bad, sometimes," he said simply and waited. Last night—if things came out right later—will have been just what Elinor needed most, he decided privately. She had always struck him as being a little too aloof to be quite human—but she was changing under his eyes to a very human variety of worried young girl.

"Well, isn't there something we can really *do*?" she said diffidently, then changing,

"Oh I mean it—if you don't think it's only—probing—asking that?" as she changed again.

"Not a thing I'm afraid, Elinor, though I really do thank you." He hated his voice—it sounded so brave. "It's just finished, that's all. Can't kick very well. Oh no," as she started to speak, "it doesn't hurt to talk about, really. Helps, more. And Peter and Ted help too—especially Ted."

He watched her narrowly—changing color like that must mean a good deal with Elinor.

Then "Why Ted?" she said, almost as if she were talking to herself and then started to try and make him see that that didn't matter—a spectacle to which he remained gratifiedly blind. He addressed his next remarks at the dish of jam so that she wouldn't be able to catch his eye.

"Oh, I'm not slamming Peter's sympathetic soul, El, you know I'm not—but Ted and I just happened to go through such a lot of the war and after it together—and then Ted saw a good deal more of Nancy. Peter's delightful. And kind. But he does assume that because lots of people get engaged and disengaged again all over the lot these days as if they were cutting for bridge-partners there isn't anything particularly serious in things like that. Nothing to really make you make faces and bust, that is. Well, ours happened to be one of the other kind—that's the difference. And Peter, well, Peter isn't exactly the soul of constancy when it comes to such matters—"

"Peter—oh Peter—if you knew the millions of girls that Peter's kept pictures of—"

"Well, I've heard all about the last hundred thousand or so, I think. But there's perfect safety in thousands. It's when you start being so stalwart and sure and manly about one—"

Oliver spread out his hands. Elinor's color—the way it fluctuated at least—was most encouraging. So was the fact that she had tried to butter her last muffin with the handle of her knife. "But I don't see *how* if a girl really cared about a man she could let anything—" she said and then stopped with a burning flush. And now Oliver knew that he had to be very careful. He looked over his tools and decided that infantile bitterness was best.

"Girls are girls," he said shortly, stabbing a muffin. "They tell you they do and then they tell you they don't—that's them."

"Oliver Crowe, I never heard such a nasty, childish seventeen-year-old idea from you in my whole life!" Oh what would calm Mrs. Piper say if she could see Elinor, eyes cloudy with anger, leaning across the tea-wagon and emphasizing her points by waves of a jammy knife as she defends constancy and romance! "They do *not*! When a girl cares for a man—and she knows he cares for her—she doesn't care about *anything* else, she—"

"That's what Nancy said," remarked Oliver placidly out of his muffin. "And then—"

"Well, you know I'm sorry for you—you know I'm just as sorry for you as I can be," went on Elinor excitedly. "But all the same, my dear Ollie, you have no right in the least to say that just because one girl has broken her engagement with you, all girls are the same. I know dozens of girls—" "So do I," from Oliver, quietly. "Dozens. And they're just the same."

"They *aren't*. And I haven't the slightest wish to suggest that it was *your* fault, Oliver—but no girl as sweet and friendly and darling as Nancy Ellicott, the little I knew of her that is, but other girls can tell, and she certainly thought you were the person that made all the stars come out in the sky and twinkle, would go and break her engagement *entirely* of her own accord—you *must* have—"

And now Oliver looked at her with a good deal of sorrowful pity—she had delivered herself so completely into his hands.

"I never said it was her fault, Elinor," he said gently, keeping the laughter back by a superb effort of will. "It was mine, I am sure," and then he added most sorrowfully, "All mine."

"*Well!*"

For a moment he forgot that he was there playing checkers with himself and Elinor for Ted.

"You've never been through it, have you?" he said rather

fiercely. "You can't have—you couldn't talk like that if you had. When you've put everything you've got in mind or body or soul completely in one person's hands and then, just because of a silly misunderstanding we neither of us meant—they drop it—and you drop with it and the next thing you know you're nothing but a *mess* and all you can wonder is if even the littlest part of you will ever feel whole again—" He realized that he was very nearly shouting, and then, suddenly, that if he kept on this way the game was over and lost. He must think about Ted, not Nancy. Ted, Ted. Mr. Theodore Billett, Jr.

"She'd forgiven me such a lot," he ended rather lamely. "I thought she'd keep on."

But his outburst had only made Elinor feel the sorrier for him—he felt like a burglar as he saw the kindness in her eyes.

"I don't imagine she ever had such an awful lot to forgive, Ollie," she said gently.

Then the lie he had been leading up to all the way came at last, magnificently hesitant.

"She had, Elinor. I was in France you know."

He was afraid when he had said it—it sounded so much like a title out of a movie—but he looked steadily at her and saw all the color go out of her face and then return to it burningly.

"Well, that wasn't anything to be—forgiven about exactly—was it?" she said unsteadily.

He spoke carefully, in broken sentences, only the knowledge that this was the only way he could think of to help things nerving his mind. "It wasn't being in France, Elinor. It was—the adjuncts. I don't suppose I was any worse than most of my outfit—but that didn't make it any easier when I had to tell her I hadn't been any better. I felt," his voice rose, his literary trick of mind had come to his rescue now and made him know just how he would have felt if it had really happened, "I felt as if I were in hell. Really. But I had to tell her. And when she'd forgiven me that—and said that it was all right—that it didn't make any real difference now—I thought she was about the finest person in the world—for telling me such nice lies. And after that—I was so sure that it was all right—that because of her knowing and still being able to care—it would last—oh well—"

He stopped, waiting for Elinor but Elinor for a person so voluble a little while ago seemed curiously unwilling to speak.

"Lord knows why I'm telling you this—except that we started arguing and you're nice enough to listen. It's not tea-table conversation, or it wouldn't have been ten years ago—and if I've shocked you, I'm sorry. But after that, as I said—I didn't think there was anything that could separate us—really I didn't—and then just one little time when we didn't quite understand each other and—over. Sorry to spoil your illusions, Elinor, but that's the way people do."

"But how could she?" and this time there was nothing but pure hurt questioning in Elinor's voice and the words seemed to hurt her as if she were talking needles. "Why Ollie—she couldn't possibly—if she really cared—"

All he wondered was which of them would break first.

"She could," he said steadily, in spite of the fact that everything in his mind kept saying "No. No. No." "Any girl could—easily. Even you, Elinor—if you'll excuse my being rude—"

For a moment he thought that his carefully plotted scenario was going to break up into melodrama with the reticent, composed and sympathetic Elinor's suddenly rising and slapping his face. Then he heard her say in a voice of utter anger, "How can you say anything like that, how can you? You are being the most hateful person that ever lived. Why if I really cared for anyone—if I ever really cared—" and then she began to cry most steadily and whole-heartedly into her napkin and Oliver in spite of all the generous plaudits he was receiving from various parts of his mind for having carried delicate business successfully to a most dramatic conclusion, wondered what in the name of Hymen his cue was now. Some remnants of diplomacy however kept him from doing anything particularly obtrusive and, after he had received an official explanation of nervous headache with official detachment, the end of tea found them being quite cheerful together. Neither alluded directly to what both thought about most but in spite of that each seemed inwardly convinced of being completely if cryptically understood by the other and when the noise of the first returning motor brought a friendly plotter's "You talk to them—they mustn't see me this way," from Elinor and a casual remark from Oliver that he felt sure he would have to run into town for dinner—family had forwarded a letter from an editor this morning—so if she wanted anything done—they seemed to comprehend each other very thoroughly.

He babbled with the returning jazzers for a quarter of an hour or so, tactfully circumvented Peter into offering him the loan of a car since he had to go into New York, and intimated that he would drop back and in at the Rackstraws' dance as soon as possible, after many apologies for daring to leave at all. Then he went slowly upstairs, humming loudly as he did so. Elinor met him outside his door.

"Ollie—as long as you're going in—I wonder if you'd mind—" Her tone was elaborately careless but her eyes were dancing as she gave him a letter, firmly addressed but unstamped.

"No, glad to—" And then he grinned. "You'll be at the Rackstraws'."

"Yes, Ollie."

"Well—we'll be back by ten thirty or try to. Maybe earlier," he said at her back and she turned and smiled once at him. Then he went into his room.

"Mr. Theodore Billett," said the address on the letter, "252A Madison Ave., N. Y. C.," and down in the lower corner, "Kindness of Mr. Oliver Crowe."

He thought he might very well ask for the latter phrase on Ted's and Elinor's wedding invitations. He passed a hand over his forehead—that had been harder than walking a tight-rope with your head in a sack—but the chasm had been crossed and nothing was left now but the fireworks on the other side. How easy it was to tinker other people's love-affairs for them—for oneself the difficulties were somehow a little harder to manage, he thought. And then he began considering how long it would take from Southampton to New York in the two-seater and just where Ted would most likely be.

XXXIII

A long-distance telephone conversation about six o'clock in the afternoon between two voices usually so even and composed that the little pulse of excitement beating through both as they speak now seems perilous, unnatural. One is Mr. Severance's thin cool speech and the other—most curious, that—seems by every obsequious without being servile, trained and impassive turn and phrase to be that of that treasure among household treasures, Elizabeth.

"My instructions were that I was to call you, sir, whenever I was next given an evening out."

"Yes, Elizabeth. Well?"

"I have been given an evening out tonight, sir."

"Yes."

"Mrs. Severance has told me that I am on no account to return till tomorrow morning, sir."

"Yes. Go on."

"There are the materials of a small but quite sufficient meal for two persons in the refrigerator, sir. Mrs. Severance is dining out, sir—she said." "Yes. Any further information?"

"Mrs. Severance received a telephone call this morning, sir, before she went out. It was after that that she told me I was to have the evening."

"You did not happen to—overhear—the conversation, did you, Elizabeth?"

"Oh no, sir. Mrs. Severance spoke very low. The only words that I could catch were 'You' at the beginning and 'Please come' near the end. The words 'please come' were rather—affectionately—spoken if I might make so bold, sir."

"You have done very well, Elizabeth."

"Thank you, sir."

"There is nothing else?"

"No, sir. Should you wish me to 'phone you again before tomorrow morning, sir?"

"No, Elizabeth."

"Thank you, sir. Good-by, sir."

"Good-by, Elizabeth."

Stephen Vincent Benet

XXXIV

The rest of the party has scattered to the gardens or the porch—Oliver has wandered into the library alone to wait for Peter who is bringing around the two-seater himself. It is a big dim room with books all the way up to the ceiling and a comfortable leather lounge upon which he sinks, picks up a magazine from a little table beside it and starts ruffling the pages idly. The chirrup of a telephone bell that seems to come out of the wall beside him makes him jump.

Then he remembers—that must be Mr. Piper's office through the closed door there. He remembers, as well, Peter joking with his father once about his never getting away from business even in the country and pointing at the half dozen telephones on top of the big flat desk with a derisive gesture while detailing to Oliver the fondness that Sargent Piper has for secretive private wires and the absurd precautions he takes to keep them intensely private. "Why he went and had all his special numbers here changed once just because I found out one of them by mistake and called him up on it for a joke— the cryptic old person!" Peter had said with mocking affection.

The telephone chirrups again and Oliver gets up and goes toward the door of the office with a vague idea of answering it since there seem to be no servants about. Then he remembers something else—Peter's telling him that nothing irritates his father more than having anyone else answer one of his private wires—and stops with his hand on the door that has swung inward an inch or so already under his casual pressure. It

doesn't matter anyhow—there—somebody has answered it—
Mr. Piper probably, as there is another door to the office and
both of them are generally kept locked. Mr. Piper like all great
business men has his petty idiosyncrasies.

Oliver is just starting to turn away when a whisper of sound
that seems oddly like "Mrs. Severance" comes to his ear by
some trick of acoustics through the door. He hesitates—and
stays where he is, wondering all the time why he is doing
anything so silly and unguest-like—and also what on earth he
could say if Mr. Piper suddenly flung open the door. But Ted
has told him a good deal at various times of the more
mysterious aspects of Mrs. Severance, and her name jumping
out at him this way from the middle of Mr. Piper's private
office makes it rather hard to act like a copybook gentleman—
especially with his last conversation with Ted still plain in his
mind.

The voices are too low for him to hear anything distinctly but
again one of the speakers says "Mrs. Severance"—of that he is
entirely sure. The receiver clicks back and Oliver regains the
lounge in three long soft strides, thanking his carelessness that
he is still wearing rubber-soled sport-shoes. He is very much
absorbed in an article on "Fishing for Tuna" when Peter comes
in.

"Well, Oliver, everything ready for you. Awfully sorry you
have to rush in this way—"

"Yes, nuisance all right, but it's my one best editor and that
may mean something real—terribly cheeky thing for me to do,
Pete—bumming your car like this—"

"Oh rats, you know you're welcome—and anyhow I'm
lending it to you because you'll have to bring it back, and that
means you'll come back yourself—"

"Well look, Pete, *please* make all the excuses you can for me to
your mother. And I'll run back here and change and then go

over to the Rackstraws', as soon as I can—Elinor told you about Ted?"

"Yes. Sounds sort of simple to me asking him back tonight for that beach picnic tomorrow when he absolutely had to leave this morning—but I never could keep all Elinor's social arrangements straight. Certainly hope he can get off."

"So do I," says Oliver non-committally and then the door of Mr. Piper's office opens and Mr. Piper comes out looking as well-brushed and courteous as usual but with a face that seems as if it had been touched all over lightly with a grey painful stain.

"Hello, Father? Anything up from Secret Headquarters?"

"No, boy," and Oliver is surprised at the effort with which Mr. Piper smiles. "Winthrop called up a few minutes ago about those Hungarian bonds but it wasn't anything important—" and again Oliver is very much surprised indeed, though he does not show it.

"Is your mother here, Peter?"

"Upstairs dressing, I think, Father."

Mr. Piper hesitates.

"Well, you might tell her—it's nothing of consequence but I must go in to town for a few hours—I shall have them give me a sandwich or so now and catch the 7.03, I think."

"But look, Father, Oliver has to go in too, for dinner—he's taking the two-seater now. Why don't you let him take you too—that would save time—" "Perfectly delighted to, Mr. Piper, of course, and—"

Mr. Piper looks full at Oliver—a little strangely, Oliver thinks.

"That would be—" Mr. Piper begins, and then seems to change his mind for no apparent reason. "No, I think the train would be better, I do not wish to get in too early, though I thank you, Oliver," he says with an old-fashioned bob of his head. "And now I must really—a little food perhaps"—and he escapes before either Oliver or Peter has time to argue the question. Oliver turns to Peter.

"Look here, Pete, if I'm—"

"You're not. Oh *I'd* think it'd be a lot more sensible of Father to let you take him in, but you never can tell about Father. Something must be up, though, in spite of what he says—he's supposed to be on a vacation and I haven't seen him look the way he does tonight since some of the tight squeezes in the war."

XXXV

It all started by having too much Mrs. Winters at a time, Nancy decided later. Mrs. Winters went down with comparative painlessness in homeopathic doses but Mrs. Winters day in and day out was too much like being forcibly fed with thick raspberry syrup. And then there had been walking up the Avenue from the Library alone the evening before—and remembering walks with Oliver—and coming across that copy of the "Shropshire Lad" in Mrs. Winters' bookcase and thinking just how Oliver's voice had sounded when he read it aloud to her—a process of some difficulty, she recalled, because he had tried to read with an arm around her. And then all the next day as she tried to work nothing but Oliver, Oliver, running through her mind softshoed like a light and tireless runner, crumbling all proper dignity and good resolutions away from her, little hard pebble by little hard pebble, till she had finally given up altogether, called up Vanamee and Company on the telephone and asked, with her heart in her mouth, if Mr. Oliver Crowe were there. The reply that came seemed unreal somehow—she had been so sure he would be and every nerve in her body had been so strung to wonder at what she was going to say or do when he finally answered, that the news that he had left three weeks before brought her down to earth as suddenly as if she had been tripped. All she could think of was that it must be because of her that Oliver had left the company—and illogically picture a starving Oliver painfully wandering the streets of New York and gazing at the food displayed in restaurant windows with lost and hopeless eyes.

Then she shook herself—what nonsense—he must be at Melgrove. She couldn't call him up at Melgrove, though, he mightn't be there when she 'phoned and then his family would answer and what his family must think of her now, when they'd been so perfectly lovely when she and Oliver were first engaged—she shivered a little—no, that wouldn't do. And letters never really said things—it mustn't be letters—besides, she thought, humbly, it would be so awful to have Oliver send letters back unopened. Two weeks of pure Mrs. Winters had chastened Nancy to an unusual degree.

For all that though, it was not until Mrs. Winters had left her alone for the evening after offering her an invitation to attend a little discussion group that met Wednesday evenings and read literary papers at each other, an invitation which Nancy somewhat stubbornly declined, that she finally made up her mind. Then she sighed and went to the telephone again.

"Mr. Oliver Crowe? He is away on a visit just at present but we expect him back tomorrow afternoon." Margaret is pretending for her own satisfaction over the wire that the Crowes have a maid. "Who is calling, please?"

Rather shakily, "A f-friend."

Briskly. "I understand. Well, he will be back tomorrow. Is that all that you wished to inquire? No message?"

"Good-by then," and again Nancy thinks that things simply will not be dramatic no matter how hard she tries.

She decides to take a small walk however—small because she simply must get to bed before Mrs. Winters comes back and starts talking at her improvingly. The walk seems to take her directly to the nearest Subway—and so to the Pennsylvania Station, where, after she has acquired a timetable of trains to Melgrove, she seems to be a good deal happier than she has been for some time. At least as she is going up the cake-colored stairs to the Arcade again she cannot help taking the last one with an irrepressible skip.

XXXVI

Oliver had quite a little time to think things over as the two-seater purred along smooth roads toward New York. The longer he thought them over, the less amiable some few of the things appeared. He formed and rejected a dozen more or less incredible hypotheses as to what possible connection there could be between Mrs. Severance and Sargent Piper—none of them seemed to fit entirely and yet there must be something perfectly simple, perfectly easy to explain—only what on earth could it be?

He went looking through his mind for any scraps that might possibly piece together—of course he hadn't known Peter since College without finding out that in spite of their extreme politeness toward each other, Peter's mother and father really didn't get on. Club-stories came to him that he had tried to get away from—the kind of stories that were told about any prominent man, he supposed—a little leering paragraph in "Town Gossip"—a dozen words dropped with the easy assuredness of tone that meant the speakers were alluding to something that everyone knew by people who hadn't realized that he was Peter's friend. A caustically frank discussion of Mrs. Severance with Ted in one of Ted's bitter moods—a discussion that had given Oliver a bad half-hour later with Louise.

But things like that didn't *happen*—people whose houses you stayed at—people your sister brought home over the week-end—the fathers of your own friends. And then Oliver winced

Stephen Vincent Benet

as he remembered the afternoon when all the New Haven evening papers had screamed with headlines over the Witterly divorce suit—and Bob Witterly's leaving College because he couldn't stand it—that had been people you knew all right— and everyone had always had such a good time at the Witterlys' too.

It was all perfectly incredible of course—but he would have to find Ted just as soon as possible, no matter where he had to go to find him—and as the little reel of the speedometer began to hitch toward the left and into higher figures, Oliver felt very relieved indeed that he had the two-seater and that Mr. Piper wasn't coming into town till the 7.03.

He got into New York to find he hadn't made as good time as he'd thought—a couple of traffic blocks had kept him back for valuable minutes—though of course the minutes couldn't be valuable exactly when it was all bosh about his having to get in so quickly after all. He went first to 252A Madison Avenue, hoping most heartily that Ted would be there on the fifth floor with his eyeshade over his eyes and large law-books crowding his desk, but the door was locked and knockings brought no response except a peevish voice from the other side of the narrow hall requesting any gentleman that was a gentleman to shut up for Gawd's sake. The Yale Club next—there was just a chance that Ted might be there—

Oliver went through the Yale Club a good deal more thoroughly than most pages, from the lobby to the upstairs dining-room. He even invaded the library to the suspicious annoyance of some old uncle who was pretending to read a book held upside down in his lap in order to camouflage his pre-prandial nap. No Ted—though half-a-dozen acquain-tances who insisted on saying hello and taking up time. Back to the street and a slight dispute with a policeman as regarded the place where Oliver had parked his car. He looked at his watch just before poking the self-starter—Mr. Piper's train must be halfway to New York by now. He set his lips and turned down 44th Street toward the Avenue.

Fourth floor Ted had said. The elevator went much too quickly for Oliver—he was standing in front of a most non-committal door-bell before he had arranged the racing tumult of thought in his mind enough to be in any measure sure of just what the devil he was going to say.

Moreover he was oppressed by a familiar and stomachless sensation—the sensation he always had when he tried to high-dive and stood looking gingerly down from a shaky platform at water that seemed a thousand miles away and as flat and hard as a blue steel plate. There wasn't any guide in any Manual of Etiquette he had ever heard of on What to Say When Interrupting a Tete-a-Tete between Your Best Friend and a Dangerous And Beautiful Woman. He wondered idly if Ted would ever speak to him again—Mrs. Severance certainly wouldn't—and he rather imagined that even if Ted and Elinor did get married he would hardly be the welcome guest he had always expected to be there.

Well, that was what you get for trying to pull a Jonathan when the Saul in question was behaving a good deal more like David in the affair with Uriah the Hittite's spouse—and it wasn't safe and Biblical and all done with a couple of thousand years ago but abashingly real and now happening directly under your own astonished eyes. He licked his lips a little nervously—they seemed to be rather dry. No use standing outside the door like a wooden statue of Unwelcome Propriety anyhow—the thing had to be done, that was all—and he pushed the bell-button with all the decision he could force into his finger.

The fact that it was not answered at once helped him a good deal by giving him a certain strength of annoyance. He pushed again.

It was Mrs. Severance who answered it finally—and the moment he saw her face he knew with an immense invisible shock of relief how right he had been, for it was composed as an idol's but under the composure there was emotion, and, the moment she saw him, anger, as strong and steady and impassive as the color of a metal that is only white because it has been possessed to extremity already with all the burning heat that its substance can bear. She was dressed in some stuff that moved with her and was part of her as wholly as if it and her body had been made together out of light and gilded cloud—he had somehow never imagined that she could be as—lustrous—as that—it gave him the sensation that he had only seen her before when she was unlighted like an empty lantern, and that now there was such fire of light in her that the very glass that contained it seemed to be burning of itself. And then he realized that she had given him good-evening with an exquisite politeness, shaken hands and now was obviously waiting, with a little tired look of surprise around her mouth, to find out exactly why he was there at all.

He gathered his wits—it wasn't fair, somehow, for her to be wearing that air of delicate astonishment at an unexpected call at dinner-time when he hadn't been invited—it forced him into being so casually polite.

"Sorry to break in on you like this, Mrs. Severance," he said with a ghastly feeling that after all he might be entirely wrong, and another that it was queer to have to be so formal, in the afternoon tea sense, with his words when his whole mind was boiling with pictures of everything from Ted as a modern Tannhauser in a New York Venusberg to triangular murder. "I hope I'm not—disturbing you?"

"Oh no. No," and he suddenly felt a most complete if unwilling admiration for the utter finish with which she was playing her side of the act.

"Only you see," and this was Oliver doing his best at the ingenuous boy, "Ted Billett, you know—he said he might be having dinner with you this evening—and I've got a very important letter for him—awful nuisance—don't see why it couldn't have gone in the mail by itself—but the man was absolutely insistent on my delivering it by hand." "A letter? Oh yes. And they want an answer right away?" Again Oliver realized grudgingly that whatever Mrs. Severance might be she was certainly not obvious. For "I'm so glad you came then," she was saying with what seemed to be perfect sincerity. "Won't you come in?"

That little pucker that came and went in the white brow meant that she was sure that she could manage him, sure she could carry it off, Oliver imagined—and he was frank enough with himself to admit that he was not at all sure that she couldn't.

"Oh Ted—" he heard her say, very coolly but also with considerable distinctness, as if her voice had to carry, "there's a friend of yours here with a letter for you—"

And then she had brought him inside and was apologizing for having the front room so badly lighted but one had to economize on light-bills, didn't one, even for a small apartment, and besides didn't it give one a little more the real feeling of evening? And Oliver was considering why, when if as he pressed the bell, he had felt so much like a modern St. George and wholly as if he were doing something rather fine and perilous, he should feel quite so much like a gauche seventeen-year-old now. He thought that he would not enjoy playing chess with Mrs. Severance. She was one of those people who smiled inoffensively at the end of a game and then said they thought it would really be a little evener if they gave you both knights.

Ted reassured him though. Ted, stumbling out of the dining-room, with a mixture of would-be unconcern, compound embarrassment and complete though suppressed fury at Oliver on his face. It was hardly either just or moral, Oliver reflected, that Mrs. Severance should be the only one of them to seem completely at her ease.

"Hello, Ollie," in the tone of "And if you'd only get the hell out as quickly as possible." "Mrs. Severance—" a stumble over that. "You've got a letter for me?"

Stephen Vincent Benet

"Yes. It's important," said Oliver as firmly as he could. He gave it, and, as Ted sat down near a lamp to read it, Oliver saw by one sudden momentary flash that passed over Mrs. Severance's face that she had seen the address and known instantly that the handwriting was not that of a man. And then Oliver began to think that he might have been right when he had thought of the present expedition as something rather perilous—he found that he had moved three steps away from Mrs. Severance without his knowing it, very much as he might have from an unfamiliar piece of furniture near which he was standing and which had instantaneously developed all the electric properties of a coil of live wire. Then he looked at Ted's face—and what he saw there made him want to kick himself for looking—because it is never proper for even the friendliest spectator to see a man's private soul stripped naked as a grass-stalk before his own eyes. It was horribly like watching Ted lose balance on the edge of a cliff that he had been walking unconcernedly and start to fall without crying out or any romantic gestures, with only that look of utter surprise struck into his face and the way his hands clutched as if they would tear some solid hold out of the air. Oliver kept his eyes on him in a frosty suspense while he read the letter all through three times and then folded it and put it carefully away in his breast pocket—and then when he looked at Mrs. Severance Oliver could have shouted aloud with immense improper joy, for he knew by the way Ted's hands moved that they were going back in the car together.

Ted was on his feet and his voice was as grave as if he were apologizing for having insulted Mrs. Severance in public, but under the meaninglessness of his actual words it was wholly firm and controlled.

"I'm awfully sorry—I've got to go right away. You'll think me immensely rude but it's something that's practically life-and-death." "Really?" said Mrs. Severance and Oliver could have clapped his hands at her accent. Now that the battle had ended bloodlessly, he supposed he might be permitted to applaud, internally at least. And "I'm sorry—but this is over," said every note in Ted's voice and "Lost have I? Well then——" every note in hers.

It occurred to Oliver that things were badly arranged—all this—and he was the only audience.

Life seemed sudden lavish in giving him benefit performances of other people's love-affairs—he supposed it was all part of the old and deathless jest.

And then, like a prickling of cold, there passed over him once more that little sense of danger. Mrs. Severance and Ted were both standing looking at each other and neither was saying anything—and Ted looked by his face as if he were walking in his sleep.

"The car's down below, old boy," said Oliver helpfully, and then, a little louder "Peter's car, you know," and whatever cobwebs had been holding Ted for the last instant broke apart. He went over to Mrs. Severance. "Good-by."

"Good-by," and he started making apologies again while she merely looked and Oliver was suddenly fretting like a weary hostess whose callers have stayed hours too long, to have him down in the car and the car pointed again with its nose toward Southampton.

And then he heard, through Ted's last apologia, the whir of a mounting elevator.

The elevator couldn't stop at the fourth floor—it couldn't. But it did, and there was the noise of the gate slung back and "*What's that?*" said Mrs. Severance sharply, her politeness broken to bits for the first time.

They were all standing near the door, and, with a complete disbelief in all that he was hearing and seeing, Oliver heard Mrs. Severance's voice in his ear, "The kitchen—fire-escape—" saw her push Ted toward him as if she were shifting a piece of cumbrous furniture, and obeyed her orders implicitly because he was too surprised to think of doing anything else.

He hurried himself and the still half-somnambulistic Ted through the dining-room curtains, just in time to catch a last glimpse of Mrs. Severance softly pressing with all her weight and strength against her side of the door of the apartment as a man's quick short footsteps crossed the hall in two strides, and after a second's pause, a key clicked into the lock.

XXXVII

Mrs. Severance, her whole weight against the door, felt it push at her fiercely without opening, and, even in the midst of her turmoil, smiled. Mr. Severance had never been exactly what one would call an athlete—

She slackened her pressure, little by anxious little. Her hand crept down to the knob, then she jerked it sharply and stood back and Mr. Piper came stumbling into the room, a little too fast for dignity. He had to catch to her to save himself from falling but as soon as he had recovered his balance he jerked his hands away from her as if they had taken hold of something that hurt him and when he stood up she saw that his face was grey all over and that his breath came in little hard sniffs through his nose.

"Sorry, Sargent," she said easily. "I heard your key but that silly old door is sticking again. You didn't hurt yourself, did you?"

For an instant she thought that everything was going to be perfectly simple—his face had changed so, with an intensity of relief almost childish, at the sound of her accustomed voice. Then the greyness came back.

"Do you mind—introducing me—Rose—to the gentleman— you are dining with tonight?" he said with a difficulty of speech as if actual words were not things he was accustomed to using. "I merely—called—to be quite sure."

She managed to look as puzzled as possible.

"The gentleman?"

"Oh yes, the gentleman." He seemed neither to be particularly disgusted nor murderously angry—only so utterly tired in body and spirit that she thought oddly that it seemed almost as if any sudden gesture or movement might crumble him into pieces of fine grey paper at her feet.

"Oh, there isn't any use in pretending, Rose—any more. I have my information."

"Yes? From whom?"

"What on earth does it matter? Elizabeth—since you choose to know."

"Elizabeth," said Mrs. Severance softly. She could not imagine how time, even when successfully played for and gained, could help the situation very much—but that was the only thing she could think of doing, and she did it, therefore, with every trick of deliberation she knew, as if any instant saved before he went into the dining-room might bring salvation.

"Do you know, I was always a little doubtful about Elizabeth. She was a little too beautifully incurious about everything to be quite real—and a little too well satisfied with her place, even on what we paid her. But of course is she has been supplementing her salary with private-detective work for you—"

She shrugged her shoulders.

"I suppose you were foolish enough to give her one of your private numbers," she said a trifle acidly. "Which will mean that you will be paying her a modest blackmail all the rest of your life, and you'll probably have to provide for her in your will. Oh, I know Elizabeth! She'll be perfectly secret—if she's paid for it—she'll never make you willing to risk the scandal by asking for more than just enough. But if this is the way you carry on all your confidential investigations, Sargent—well, it's fortunate you have large means—"

"She doesn't know who I am."

"Oh Sargent, Sargent! When all she has to do is to subscribe to 'Town and Country.' Or call up the number you gave her, some time, and ask where it is."

"There are the strictest orders about nobody but myself ever answering the telephones in my private office."

"And servants are always perfectly obedient—and there are no stupid ones—and accidents never happen. Sargent, really—"

"That doesn't matter. I didn't come here to talk about Elizabeth." "Really? I should think you might have. I could have given you all the information you required a good deal less expensively—and now, I suppose, I'll have to think up some way of getting rid of Elizabeth as well. I can't pay her off with one of my new dresses this time—"

"*Who is he?*"

"Suppose we start talking about it from the beginning, Sargent—?"

"*Where* is he?"

"In the dining-room, I imagine. It wouldn't be very well bred of anyone, would it, to come out and be introduced in the middle of this very loud, very vulgar quarrel that you are making with me—"

"I'm going to see."

"No, Sargent."

"Let me pass, Rose!"

"I will not. Sargent, I will not let you make an absolute fool of yourself before my friends before you give me a chance to explain—"

"I will, I tell you! I will! *Let me go!*"

They were struggling undignifiedly in the center of the room, her firm strong hands tight over his wrists as he pawed at her, trying to wrench himself away. Mr. Piper was a gentleman no longer—nor a business man—nor a figure of nation-wide importance—he was only a small furious figure with a face as grey and distorted as a fighting ape's who was clutching at the woman in front of him as if he would like to tear her with his hands. A red swimming had fallen over his eyes—all he knew was that the woman-person in front of him had fooled him more bitterly and commonly than anyone had been fooled since Adam—and that if he could not get loose in some way or other from the hateful strength that was holding him, he would burst into the disgusting tears of a vicious small boy who is being firmly held down and spanked by an older girl. Grammar, manners and sense had gone from him as completely as if he had never possessed them.

"Lemme go! oh damn you, damn you—you *woman*—you *devil—lemme* go!"

"Be *quiet,* Sargent! Oh shut up, you *fool, shut up!*"

A noise came from the kitchen—a noise like the sound of a man falling over boxes. Mr. Piper struggled furiously—Paris was crawling out of the window—Paris, the sleek, sly chamberer, the gay hateful cuckoo of his private nest was getting away! Mrs. Severance turned her head toward the noise a second. Mr. Piper fought like a crippled wrestler.

"Grr-ah! Ah, would you, would you?"

He had wrenched one hand free for an instant—it went to his pocket and came out of it with something that shone and was hard like a new metal toy.

"Now will you lemme go?" But Mrs. Severance tried to grab for the hand with the revolver in it instead, and succeeded only in striking the barrel a little aside. There was a noise that sounded like a cannon-cracker bursting in Mr. Piper's face—it was so near—and then he was standing up, shaking all over, but free and a man ready to explain a number of very painful things to Paris as soon as he caught him. He took one step toward the dining-room, sheer rage tugging at his body as high wind tugs at a bough. Now that woman was out of the way—

And then he saw that she was out of the way indeed. She could not have fallen without his hearing her fall—how could she?— but she was lying on the floor in a crumple of clothes and one of her arms was thrown queerly out from her side as if it did not belong to her body any longer. He stood looking at her for what seemed one long endless wave of uncounted time and that firecracker noise he had heard kept echoing and echoing through his head like the sound of loud steps along a long and empty corridor. Then he suddenly dropped the pistol and knelt clumsily beside her.

"Rose! Rose!" he started calling huskily, his hands feeling with frantic awkwardness for her pulse and her heart, as Oliver Crowe ran into the room through the curtains.

Stephen Vincent Benet

XXXVIII

Oliver thought that he had never been quite so sure of anything as he was that he must be insane. He was insane. Very shortly some heavy person in uniform would walk into the tidy kitchen where he and Ted were crouching like moving-picture husbands and remark with a kind smile that the Ahkoond of Whilom was giving a tea-party in the Mountains of the Moon that afternoon and that unless Oliver (or, as he was probable better known) St. Oliver, came back at once in the nice private car with the wire netting over its windows, everybody from God the Father Almighty to Carrie Chapman Catt would be highly displeased. For a moment Oliver thought of lunatic asylums almost lovingly—they had such fine high walls and smooth green lawns and you were so perfectly safe there from anything ever happening that was real. Then he jumped—that must be Mrs. Severance opening the door.

"What are we going to *do*?" he said to Ted in a fierce whisper.

Ted looked at him stupidly. "Do? When I don't know whether I'm on my feet or my head?" he said. His drugged passiveness showed Oliver with desolating clarity that anything that could be done would have to be done by himself. He crept over toward the window with a wild wish that black magic were included in a Yale curriculum—the only really sensible thing he could think of doing would be for both of them to vanish through the wall.

"Look! Fire-escape!"

"What?"

"*Fire-escape!*"

"All right. You take it."

Oliver had been sliding the window up all the while, cursing softly and horribly at each damnatory creak. Yes—there it was—and people thought fire-escapes ugly. Personally, Oliver had seldom seen anything in his life which combined concrete utility with abstract beauty so ideally as that little flight of iron steps leading down the entry outside the window into blackness.

"You first, Ted."

"Can't." The word seemed to come despairingly out of the bottom of his stomach.

"Came here. Own accord. Got to see it through. Take my medicine."

"You fool, she doesn't want you here! Think of Elinor!" For a moment Oliver thought Ted was going to blaze into more blind rage. Then he checked himself.

"I am. But listen to that."

The voices that came to them from the living-room were certainly both high and excited—and the second that Oliver heard one of them he knew that all his most preposterous suppositions on the drive down from Southampton had come preposterously and rather ghastly true.

"Well, *listen* to it! Do you know who the man is now? And will you get out on the fire-escape, you *fool?*"

Ted listened intently for the space of a dozen seconds. Then "Oh my God!" he said and his head went into his hands. Oliver crept over to him.

"Ted, listen—oh listen, damn you! What's the use of acting the chivalrous fool, *now*? Don't you see? Don't you understand? Don't you get it that if you leave she can explain it some way or other—that all you're doing by staying is ruining yourself and Elinor for a point of honor that hasn't any honor *to* it?"

"Oh sure. Sure. But listen to him—why great God, Ollie, if he has a gun he might kill her—probably will—Don't you see it's just because I hate the whole business now—and her—and myself—th'at I've got to stick it out? You go, Ollie, it's none of your business—"

"You go. You blessed idiot, there's no use of both of us smashing. If anybody's got to stay—I can bluff it out a good deal better than you can—trust me—"

"Oh rats. Not that it isn't very decent of you, Ollie, it is—and you'd do it—but I wouldn't even be a *person* to let you—"

They were both on their feet, talking in jerks, ears strained for every sound from that other room.

"It's *perfectly* simple—nobody's going to pull any gunplay—good Lord, imagine poor old Mr. Piper—" said Oliver uncertainly, and then as noises came to them that meant more than just talking, "*Get down that fire-escape!*"

"I can't. Let go of me, Ollie. I mustn't Listen—something's up—something bad! Get out of the way there, Ollie, I've got to go in! It *isn't* your funeral!"

"Well, it isn't going to be yours!" said Oliver through shut teeth—Ted's last remark had, somehow been a little too irritating. He thought savagely that there was only one way of dealing with completely honorable fools—Ted shouldn't, by the Lord!—Oliver had gone to just a little too much trouble in the last dozen hours to build Ted a happy home to let any of Ted's personal wishes in the matter interrupt him now. He stepped back with a gesture of defeat but his feet gripped at the floor like a boxer's and his eyes fixed burningly on the point of Ted's jaw. Wait a split-second—he wasn't near enough—now—*there*!

His fist landed exactly where he had meant it to and for an instant he felt as if he had broken all the bones in his hand. Ted was back against the wall, his mouth dropping open, his whole face frozen like a face caught in a snapshot unawares to a sudden glare of immense and ludicrous astonishment. Then he began to give at the knees like a man who has been smitten with pie in a custard-comedy and Oliver recovered from his surprise at both of them sufficiently to step in and catch him as he slumped, face forward.

He laid him carefully down on the floor, trying feverishly to remember how long a knockout lasted. Not nearly long enough, anyway. Ropes. A gag. His eyes roved frantically about the kitchen. *Towels*!

He was filling Ted's mouth with clean dish-rag and thinking dully that it was just like handling a man in the last stages of alcohol—the body had the same limp refractory heaviness all over—when he heard something that sounded like the bursting of a large blown-up paper bag from the other room. He accepted the fact with neither surprise nor curiosity. Mr. Piper had shot Mrs. Severance. Or Mrs. Severance had shot Mr. Piper. That was all.

As soon as he had safely disposed of Ted—for an eery moment he had actually considered stowing him away in a drawer of the kitchen-cabinet—it might be well to go in and investigate the murder.

And then either Mrs. Severance or Mr. Piper—whichever it

was of the two that remained alive—might very well shoot him unless he or she had shot himself or herself first. It seemed to Oliver that the latter event would save everyone a great deal of trouble.

He did not relish the idea of being left alone in a perfectly strange apartment with two corpses and one gagged, bound and unconscious best friend—but he liked the picture of himself trying to make explanations to either his hostess or Mr. Piper when, in either case, the other party to the argument would be in possession of a loaded revolver, still less. He hoped that if Mrs. Severance were the survivor she had had a sufficiently Western upbringing at least to know how to shoot. He had no particular wish to die—but anything was better than being mangled—and a reminiscence of Hedda Gabler's poet's technique with firearms caused his stomach to contract quite painfully as he tightened the knots around Ted's ankles. Ted was the devil and all to get out on the fire-escape—and then you had to tie him so that he wouldn't roll off.

He crawled back through the window, dusted his trousers, and settled his necktie as carefully as if he were going to be married. Married. And he had hoped, he thought rather pitiably, that even though Nancy had so firmly decided to blight him forever she might have a few pleasant memories of their engagement at least. Instead—well, he could see the headlines now. "Big Financier, Youth and Mystery Woman Die in Triple Slaying." "*Dead*—Oliver Crowe, Yale 1917, of Melgrove, L. I."

It hadn't been his job, damn it, it hadn't been his job at all. It was now, though, with Ted perfectly helpless on the fire-escape where any crazy person could take pot-shots at him as if he were a plaster pipe in a shooting gallery. The idea of escape had somehow never seriously occurred to him—what had happened in the evening already had impressed him so with a sense of inane fatality that he could not even conceive of the possibility of any-thing's coming right. In any event, Ted, tied up the way he was, was too heavy and clumsy to carry down even the most ordinary flight of stairs—and if he were going to be shot, he somehow preferred to gasp his last breaths out on a comfortably carpeted floor rather than clinging like a disreputable spider to the iron web of a fire-escape.

Oliver sighed—Nancy's firmness had admittedly quite ruined all the better things in life—but even the merest sort of mere existence had got to be, at times, a rather pleasant convention—how pleasant, he felt, he had never quite realized somehow until just now. Then, with a vague idea of getting whatever was to happen over with as quickly and decently as possible, he settled his tie once more and trotted meekly through the dining-room and beyond the curtains.

XXXIX

"Why, Mr. Piper!" was Oliver's first and wholly inane remark.

It was not what he had intended to say at all—something rather more dramatic and on the lines of "Shoot if you must this old grey head, but if you will only listen to a reasonable explanation—" had been uppermost in his mind. But the sight of Peter's father crouched over what must be Mrs. Severance's body, his weak hands fumbling for her wrist and heart, his voice thin with a senile sorrow as if he had been stricken at once and in an instant with a palsy of incurable age, brought the whole world of Southampton and house-parties and reality that Oliver thought he had lost touch with forever, back to him so vividly that all he could do was gape at the tableau on the floor.

Mr. Piper looked up and for a second of relief Oliver thought that the staring eyes had not recognized him at all. Then he realized from the look in them that who or what he was made singularly little difference now to Mr. Piper. "Water!" croaked Mr. Piper. "Water! I've shot her. Oh, poor Rose, poor Rose!" and he was plucking at her dress again with absorbed, incapable fingers.

Oliver looked around him. The gun. There must have been a gun. Where? Oh *there*—and as he picked it up from under a chair he did so with much inward reverence in spite of the haste he took to it, for he felt as if it were all the next forty years of his life made little into something cold and small and of metal that he was lifting like a doll from the floor.

"Water," said Mr. Piper again and quite horribly. "Water for Rose."

It was only when he had gone back to the kitchen and started looking for glasses that he realized that Mrs. Severance might very possibly be dying out there in the other room. Till then the mere fact that he was not dying himself had been too large in his vision to give him time to develop proper sympathy for others. When he did, though, he hurried bunglingly, in spite of a nervous flash in which after accidentally touching the revolver in his pocket he almost threw it through the pane of the nearest window before he considered. A moment, though, and he was back with a spilling tumbler.

"Water," said Mr. Piper with querulous satisfaction. "Give her water." Oliver hesitated. "Where's she shot?" he said sharply.

"I don't know. Oh, I don't know. But I shot her. I shot her. Poor Rose."

It was certainly odd, there being no blood about, thought Oliver detachedly. Internal wounds? Possibly, but even so. He dipped his fingers in the glass of water, bent over Mrs. Severance and sprinkled the drops as near her closed eyelids as possible. No sound came from her and not a muscle of her body moved, but the delicate skin of the eyelids shivered momentarily. Oliver drew a long breath and stepped back.

"She's dead," said Mr. Piper. "She's dead." And he began to weep, very quietly with a mouselike sound and the slow horrible tears of age. "No use trying water on her," said Oliver loudly, and again he thought he saw the skin of the eyelids twitch a little. "Is there any brandy here—anything like that, Mr. Piper?"

"K-kitchen," said Mr. Piper with a sniff and one of his hands came away from Mrs. Severance to fumble for a key.

"I'll go get it," said Oliver, still rather loudly, and took one step away. Then he bent down again swiftly and poured the whole contents of the tumbler he was holding into the little hollow of Mrs. Severance's throat just above the collar-bone. *"Oh!"* said the dead Mrs. Severance in the tone of one who has turned on the cold in a shower unexpectedly, and she opened her eyes.

"Rose!" said Mr. Piper snifflingly. "You aren't dead? You aren't dead, dear? Rose! Rose!"

"Oh," said Mrs. Severance again, but this time tinily and with a flavor of third acts about her, and she started to relax rather beautifully into a Dying Gladiator pose.

"I'll get some more water, Mr. Piper," said Oliver briskly, and Mrs. Severance began to sit up again.

"I—fainted—silly of me," she said with a consummate dazedness. "Somebody was firing revolvers—"

"I tried—I tried—I—t-tried to s-shoot you, Rose," came from the damp little heap on the floor that was Mr. Piper.

"Really, Sargent—" said Mrs. Severance comfortably. Then she turned her head and made what Oliver was always to consider her most perfect remark. "You must think us very queer people indeed, Mr. Crowe?" she said smiling questionmgly up at him.

Oliver's smile in answer held relief beyond words. It wasn't the ordinary cosmos again—quite yet—but at least from now on he felt perfectly sure that no matter how irregular anyone's actions might become, in speech at least, every last least one of the social conventions would be scrupulously observed.

"I think—if you could help me, Sargent—" said Mrs. Severance delicately.

"Oh yes, yes, yes," from Mr. Piper very eagerly and with Oliver's and his assistance Mrs. Severance's invalid form was aided into a deep chair.

"And I think, now," she went on, "that if I could have just a little—" She let the implication float in the air like a pretty bubble. "Perhaps—it might help us all—"

"Oh *certainly*, dear," from Mr. Piper. "I—"

"In the kitchen, you said, Mr. Piper. And you must let *me*," from Oliver with complete decision. He hadn't bargained for that. Mr. Piper might not notice Ted on the fire-escape—but then again he might—and if he did he would certainly investigate—mute bound bodies were not ordinary or normal adjuncts of even the most illegal of Riverside Drive apartments. And then. Oliver's hand went down over the revolver in his pocket—if necessary he stood perfectly ready to hold up Mr. Piper at the point of his own pistol to preserve the inviolability of that kitchen.

But Mrs. Severance saved him the bother.

"If you would be so kind?" she said simply. "It's in the small cupboard—-the brown one—Sargent, you have the key?"

"Oh, yes, Rose." Mr. Piper was looking, Oliver thought, rather more embarrassed than it was fair for any man to have to look and live. His eyes kept going pitifully and always to Mrs. Severance and then creeping, away. He produced the key, however, and gave it to Oliver silently and Oliver took the first opportunity when he was through the curtains of giving whatever fates had presided over the insanities of the evening a long cheer with nine Mrs. Severances on the end.

He carefully stayed in the kitchen fifteen minutes—devoting most of the time to a cautious examination of Ted, who seemed to be gradually recovering consciousness. At least he stirred a little when poked by Oliver's foot.

"Sleeps just like a baby—oh, the sweet little fellow—the dear little fellow—" hummed Oliver wildly as he made a few last additions to the curious network of string and towels with which he had wound Ted into the fire-escape as if he had been making him a cocoon. "Well—well—*well*—what a night we're having! What a night we're having and what *will* we have next?" Then he remembered the reason for his journey and removed a bottle of brandy from the brown cup-board, found appropriate glasses and, in the ice-chest, club-soda and ginger ale. He poured himself a drink reminiscent of Paris—not that he felt he needed it for the reaction from bracing himself to die like a Pythias had left him elvishly grotesque in mind—gathered the bottles tenderly in his arms like small glass babies and went back to the living-room.

XL

And this time he was forced to pay internal high compliment to Mr. Piper as well as to Mrs. Severance. The pitiful grey image, its knees rumpled from the floor, its features streaked like a cheap paper mask with ludicrous dreadful tears, had turned back into the President of the Commercial Bank with branches in Bombay and Melbourne and all the business-capitals of the world. Not that Mr. Piper was at ease again, exactly—to be at ease under the circumstances would merely have proved him brightly inhuman—but he looked as Oliver thought he might have on one of the Street's Black Mondays when only complete firmness and complete audacity in one could keep even the Commercial afloat at a time when the Stock Exchange had turned into a floor-full of well-dressed maniacs and houses that everyone had thought as solid as granite went to pieces like sand castles.

Oliver set down the bottles and opened them with a feeling both that he had never known Mr. Piper at all before, only Peter's father, and, spookily, that neither Peter's father nor the terrible old man who had wept on the floor beside Mrs. Severance could have any real existence—this was such a complete and unemotional Mr. Piper he had before him, a Mr. Piper, too, in spite of all the oddities of the present situation, so obviously at home in his own house.

None of them said anything in particular until the mixture in the glasses had sunk about half-way down. Then Mr. Piper remarked in a pleasant voice, "I don't often permit myself—seldom even before the country adopted prohibition—but the present circumstances seem to be—er—unusual enough—to warrant—" smiled cheerfully and lifted his glass again. When he had set it down he looked at Mrs. Severance, then at Oliver, and then started to speak.

Oliver listened with some tenseness, knowing only that whatever he might possibly have imagined might happen, what would happen, to judge from the previous events of the evening, would be undoubtedly so entirely different that prophecy was no use at all. But, even so, he was not entirely prepared for the unexpectedness of Mr. Piper's first sentence.

"I feel that I owe you very considerable apologies, Oliver," the President of the Commercial began with a good deal of stateliness. "In fact I really owe you so many that it leaves me at rather a loss 'as to just how to begin." He smiled a little shyly.

"Rose has explained everything," he said, and Oliver looked at Mrs. Severance with stupefied wonder—*how?*

"But even so, there remains the difficulty—of my putting myself into words."

"Silly boy," said Mrs. Severance easily, and Oliver noted with fresh amazement that the term seemed to come from her as naturally and almost conventionally as if she had every legal American right to use it. "Let me, dear." And Oliver felt his head begin to go round like a pinwheel.

But then—but she really *couldn't* be married to Mr. Piper—and yet somehow she seemed so much more married to him than Mrs. Piper ever had been—Oliver's thoughts played fantastically for an instant over the proposition that she and Mr. Piper had been secretly converted to Mohammedanism together and he looked at Mr. Piper's grey head almost as if he expected to see a large red fez suddenly drop down upon it from the ceiling.

"No, Rose," and again Mr. Piper's voice was stately. "This is my—difficulty. No matter how hard it may be."

"Of course I did not understand—how could I?—that Rose—was such a very good friend of your sister's and all your family's. Rose had told me something about it, I believe—but I was so—foolishly disturbed—when I came in—that really, I—well I must admit that even if I had seen you when I first came in that would hardly have been the thought uppermost in my mind at the time." He spoke in the same tone of kindly reproof toward himself that he would have used if business worries had made him commit a small but definite act of inhospitality toward one of his guests.

"And naturally—you will think me very ignorant indeed of my son's affairs—and those of his friends—but while I had heard from Peter—of the breaking of your engagement—you will pardon me, I hope, if I touch upon a subject that must be so painful to you—I had no idea of the fact that you were—intending to leave the country—and knowing Rose thought that with her present position on 'Mode'—" he paused.

"It was very kind indeed of Mrs. Severance to offer to do what she could for me," said Oliver non-committally. He thought he got the drift of the story now—a sheer one enough but with Mr. Piper's present reaction toward abasement and his obvious wish to believe whatever he could, it had evidently sufficed.

"I know it was silly of me having Oliver to dinner here alone—" said Mrs. Severance with the air of one ready to apologize for a very minor impropriety. "Silly and wrong—but Louise was coming too until she telephoned about Jane Ellen's little upset—and I thought we could have such fun getting supper together with Elizabeth away. I get a little tired of *always* entertaining my friends in restaurants, Sargent, especially when I want to talk to them without having to shout. And *really* I never *imagined*—"

She looked steadily at Mr. Piper and he seemed to shrink a

Stephen Vincent Benet

little under her gaze.

"As for Elizabeth," he said with hurried vindictiveness, "Elizabeth shall leave tomorrow morning. She—"

"Oh, we might as well keep her, Sargent," said Mrs. Severance placidly. "You will have to pay her blackmail, of course—but after all that's really your fault a little, isn't it?—and it seems as if that was more or less what you had to do with any kind of passable servant nowadays. And Elizabeth is perfection—as a servant. As police—" she smiled a little cruelly. "Well, we shan't go into that, but I think it would be so much better to keep her. Then we'll be getting something out of her in return for our blackmail, don't you see?"

"Perhaps. Still we have no need of discussing that now. I can only say that if Elizabeth is to stay, she will have to—"
"Reform? My dear Sargent! When everything she did was from the most rigidly moral motives? I had no idea she was such a *clever* cat, though—"

"She will have ample opportunities of exercising her cleverness in jail if I can find any means of getting her there, and I think I can. Really," said Mr. Piper reflectively, "really when I think—"

Then he stopped.

"But you're still waiting for an—explanation—aren't you, Oliver?"

"Having been very nearly assassinated because of Elizabeth's abilities in telephone conversation, I should think he might very well be interested in knowing what is going to happen to her. However—"

"Yes," and Mr. Piper's face became very sober. He looked at his glass as if he would be willing to resign the Presidency of the Commercial in its favor if it would only explain to Oliver for him.

"You were saying, Sargent?" said Mrs. Severance implacably.

"I was. Well, I," he began, and then "You," and stopped, and then he began again.

"I said that it would be—difficult—for me to explain matters to you fully, Oliver; I find it to be—even more difficult than I had supposed. I—it is rather hard for a man of my age to defend his manner of life to one of your age, even when he himself is wholly convinced that that manner is not—unrighteous. And in this particular case, to one of his son's best friends."

He twisted his fingers around the rim of his glass. Oliver started to speak but Mr. Piper put up his hand. "No—please—it will be so much easier if I finish what I have to say first," he said rather pleadingly.

"Well—the situation here between Rose and myself—must be plain to you now." Oliver nodded, he hoped in not too knowing a way. "Plain. How that situation arose—is another matter. And a matter that would take a good deal too long to tell. Except that, given the premises from which we set forth—what followed was perhaps as inevitable as most things are in life.

"That situation has been known to no other person on earth but ourselves—all these years. And now it is known. Well, Oliver, there you have it. And you happen to have us also—entirely in your hands. Because of a spying, greedy servant—and my own stupidity and distrust—we have been completely found out. And by one of my son's best friends.

"I wish that I could apologize for—all the scene before this. Better. I hope that you will believe that I am trying to do so now. But I seldom make apologies, Oliver, even when I am evidently in the wrong—and this hasn't been one of my easiest to make. And now."

He sat back and waited, his fingers curled round his glass. And, as he looked at him, Oliver felt a little sickish, for, on the whole, he respected Mr. Piper a good deal more than his irreverent habit of mind permitted him to respect most older people, and at the same time felt pitifully sorry for him—it must be intensely humiliating to have to explain this way—and yet the only thing Oliver could do was to take the largest advantage possible of his very humiliation and straightforwardness—the truth could still do nothing at all but wreck everybody concerned.

"I give you my word of honor, Mr. Piper, to keep everything I know entirely and completely secret," said Oliver, slowly, trying to make the large words seem as little magniloquent as possible. "That's all I can say, I guess—but it's true—you can really depend on it."

"Thank you," said Mr. Piper quite simply. "I believe you, Oliver," and again Oliver felt that little burn of shame in his mind.

"Thank you," said Mrs. Severance, copying Mr. Piper finished his drink and rose. "And now, I do not wish you to misunderstand me," he said. "I have not come to my age without realizing that there are certain services that cannot be paid for. But you have done me a very great service, Oliver—a service for which I should have been glad to give nearly everything material that I possess. I merely wish you to know that in case you should ever need—assistance—from an older man—in any way—that is clumsily put, but I can think of no other suitable word at the moment—I am entirely at your disposal. Entirely so."

"Thank you, sir," said Oliver a little stiffly. Mr. Piper was certainly heaping coals of fire. Then he wondered for an instant just what Mrs. Ellicott would think if she could have heard the President of the Commercial say that to him—

Mr. Piper was moving slowly toward the door, and the politeness that had been his at the beginning of the conversation was nothing to his supreme politeness now.

"And now," he said, as if he were asking everybody's pardon for an entirely unintentional intrusion, "I really must be getting back to Southampton—and you and Rose I imagine have still quite a bit to talk over—"

"But—" said Oliver clumsily, "but Mr. Piper—" and "Must you really, dear?" said Mrs. Severance in the softest tones of conventional wifely reproach.

Her manner was ideal but Oliver somehow and suddenly felt all the admiration he had ever had for her calm power blow away from him like smoke. He could not help extremest appreciation of her utter poise—he never would be able to, he supposed—but from now on it would be the somewhat shivery appreciation that anyone with sensitive nerves might give to the smooth mechanical efficiency of a perfectly-appointed electric-chair.

"No," said Mr. Piper perfectly, "I insist. You certainly could not have finished your discussion before I came and for the present—well—it seems to me that I have intruded quite long enough. I wish it," he added and Oliver understood.

"You are staying with us, over tomorrow, Oliver, are you not?" said Mr. Piper calmly, and Oliver assented. "I suppose we shall see each other at breakfast then?"

"Oh yes, sir." And then Oliver tried to rise to Mr. Piper's magnificence of conventionality in remark. "By the way, sir, I'm driving back in Peter's car—as soon as Mrs. Severance and I have finished our talk—I couldn't pick you up anywhere, sir, could I?"

Mr. Piper smiled, consulting his watch. "There is an excellent train at 10.33—an excellent one—" he said, and again Oliver was dumfounded to realize that the whole march of events in the apartment had taken scarcely two hours.

"Thank you, Oliver, but I think I had better take that. Not that I distrust your driving in the least, but it will be fairly slow going, I imagine, over some of those roads at night—and this was one evening on which I had really intended to get a good night's sleep."

He smiled again very quaintly.

"You'll be dancing as soon as you get back, I suppose? I understand there is to be a dance this evening?"

"Yes, sir—at least, I guess so. Told Peter I'd show up."

"Youth," said Mr. Piper. "Youth." There was a certain accent of dolefulness in the way he said it.

"And now I shall call a taxi," he said briskly.

"Can't I take you down—?" Oliver began, but

"No, no. I insist," said Mr. Piper a little irritatedly, and then Oliver understood that though he might be quixotic on occasion, he was both human and—Oliver hesitated over the words, they seemed so odd to his youth to be using of a man who was certainly old enough to be his father—really in love with Mrs. Severance after all. So, until Mr. Piper's taxi came they chatted of indifferent matters much as they might have while watching people splashing about in the water from the porch of the swimming pool at Bar Harbor—and Oliver felt exceedingly in the way. These last dozen minutes were the hardest to get through of the whole evening, he thought rather dizzily; up till now he had almost forgotten about Ted, but it would be quite in keeping with everything else that had happened if just as Mr. Piper were leaving, a formal farewell on his lips and everything straightened out to everyone's conspiratorial or generously befooled satisfaction, Ted should stagger into the room like the galvanized corpse of a Pharoah wrapped in towels instead of mummy-cloth and everything from revolver-shots to a baring of inmost heart-histories would have to be gone through with again.

So when Oliver heard the telephone ring again he knew it was too good to be true, and, even when Mr. Piper started to answer it, was struck chilly with a hopeless fear that it might be police. But Fate had obviously got a trifle bored of her sport with them, or very possibly tired out by the intricacy of her previous combinations—for it was only the taxi after all and Mr. Piper was at the door.

"No use saying good-by to you now, is there, Oliver?" he said quietly, but held out his hand nevertheless.

"Well, good-by, Rose," as he scrupulously shook hands with Mrs. Severance.

"Good-by, Sargent," and then the door he had had such difficulty in opening two hours before had shut behind him and Oliver and Mrs. Severance were left looking at each other.

"Well," said Mrs. Severance with a small gasp.

"Well," said Oliver. "Well, well!"

"Excuse me," said Oliver, and he walked over to the table and poured himself what he thought as he looked at it was very like the father and mother of all drinks.

"You might—do something like that for me—" said Mrs. Severance helplessly. "If you did—I think—I might be able to think—oh, *well*."

"Well," repeated Oliver like a toast as he tipped the bottle and the drink which he poured for Mrs. Severance was so like unto his drink that it would have taken a fine millimeter-gauge to measure the difference between them.

Mrs. Severance went back to her chair and Oliver sank into the chair that had been previously occupied by Mr. Piper. As he stretched back luxuriously something small and hard and bulging made him aware of itself in his pocket. "Oh Lord, I forgot I still had that gun of Mr. Piper's!" said Oliver inconsequentially.

"Have you?" said Mrs. Severance. The fact did not seem to strike her as being of any particular importance. They both drank long and frankly and thirstily, as if they were drinking well-water after having just come in from a hot mountain trail. And again, and for a considerable time, neither spoke.

"I suppose," said Mrs. Severance finally, with a blur of delicate scorn, "I suppose our friend Mr. Billett—got away safely?"

Her words brought up a picture of Ted to Oliver,—Ted netted like a fish out there on the fire-escape, swaddled up like a great papoose in all the towels and dish-cloths Oliver had been able to find. The release was too sudden, too great—the laughter came—the extreme laughter—the laughter like a giant. He swayed in his chair, choking and beating his knees and making strange lion-like sounds.

"Ted," he gasped. "Ted! Oh, no, Mrs. Severance, Ted didn't get away! He didn't get away at all—Ted didn't! He didn't because you see he *couldn't*. He's out on the fire-escape now— oh, wait till you see him, oh Ted, oh Glory, oh what a night, what a night, what a night!"

XLI

It took a good deal of explaining, however, to make Ted understand. He was still tightly bound, though very angrily conscious when they found him and his language when Oliver removed the improvised gag was at first of such an army variety that Oliver wondered doubtfully if he hadn't better replace it until he got Ted alone. Also Oliver was forced to curse himself rather admiringly for the large number of unnecessary knots he had used, when he started to unravel his captive.

When they finally got him completely untangled Ted's first remarks were hardly those of gratitude. He declared sulkily that his head felt as if it were going to split open, that he must have a bump on the back of it as big as a squash and that it wasn't Oliver's fault if he hadn't caught pneumonia out on that fire-escape—the air, believe him, was *cold!*

Mrs. Severance, however, and as usual, rose to the occasion and produced a bottle of witch-hazel from the bathroom with which she insisted on bathing the bump till Ted remarked disgruntledly that he smelt like a hospital. Oliver watched the domestic scene with frantic laughter tearing at his vitals—this was so entirely different and unromantic an end to the evening from that from which Oliver had set out to rescue Ted like a spectacled Mr. Grundy and which Ted in his gust of madness had so bitterly and grandiosely planned.

Then they moved back into the living-room and the story was

Stephen Vincent Benet

related consecutively, by Oliver with fanciful adornments, by Mrs. Severance with a chill self-satisfaction that Oliver noticed with pleasure was like touching icicles to Ted. Ted gave his version—which only amounted to waking up on the fire-escape, trying to shout and succeeding merely in getting mouthfuls of towels—Oliver preened himself a little there—and lying there stoically and getting more and more furious until he was rescued. And while he told it he kept looking everywhere in the room but at Rose. And then Oliver remembered Mr. Piper and looked at his watch—11.04. He rose and gazed at Mrs. Severance.

"Well," he said, and then caught her eye. It was chilly, doubtless, and even by Oliver's unconventional standards he could not think of her as anything but a highly dangerous and disreputable woman—but that eye was alive with an irony and humor that seemed to him for a moment more perfect than those in any person he had ever seen. "*Must* you go?" she said sweetly. "It's been *such* an interesting party—so *original*," she hesitated. "Isn't that the word? Of course," she shrugged, "I can see that you're simply dying to get away and yet you can hardly complain that I haven't been an entertaining hostess, can you?"

"Hardly," said Oliver meekly, and Ted said nothing—he merely looked down as if his eyes were augers and his only concern in life was screwing them into the floor.

"*Must* you go?" she repeated with merciless mocking. "When it *has* been fun—and I don't suppose we'll ever see each other again in all our lives? For I can hardly come out to Melgrove now, can I, Oliver? And after you've had a quiet brotherly talk with her, I suppose I'll even have to give up lunching with Louise. And as for Ted—poor Ted—poor Mr. Billett with all his decorations of the Roller Towel, First Class—Mr. Billett must be a child that has been far too well burnt this evening, not, in any imaginable future to dread the fire?"

Both flushed, Ted deeper perhaps than Oliver, but neither

answered. There really did not seem to be anything for them to say. She moved gently toward the door—the ideal hostess. And as she moved she talked and every word she said was a light little feathered barb that fell on them softly as snowflakes and stuck like tar.

"I hope you won't mind if I send you wedding presents—both of you—oh, of course I'll be quite anonymous but it will be such a pleasure—if you'll both of you only marry nice homey girls!" Ted started at this as if he had been walking barefoot and had stepped on a wasp and she caught him instantly.

"Dear, dear, so Mr. Billett has serious intentions also—and I thought a little while ago that I was really in Mr. Billett's confidence—it only shows how little one can tell. As for Oliver, he of course is blighted—at present—but I'm sure that that will not last very long—one always finds most adequate consolation sooner or later though possibly not in the way in which one originally supposed." She sighed elfinly as Oliver muttered under his breath.

"What was that, Oliver? Oh, no, I am not at all the sort of person that writes anonymous letters to one's wife—or family—or sister," a spaced little pause between each noun. "And besides it wouldn't be much use in me, would it? for of course you young gentlemen will tell the young ladies you marry *everything* about yourselves—all honorable young people do. And then too," she spread out her hands, "to be frank. We've all been so beautifully frank about ourselves tonight— that's one thing I *have* liked so much about the evening—well, it would hardly be worth my while to take lessons in blackmailing from Elizabeth if the only subjects on which I could apply them were two impecunious young men. And, oh, I realize most perfectly—and please don't misunderstand me!—that we're all of us thieves together so to speak and only getting along on each other's sufferance. But then, if one of us ever starts telling, even a little, he or she can hardly do so in any way that will redound to anything but his or her discredit and social obliteration—how nicely I've put that!—so I don't think any of us will be very anxious to tell.

"*Good*-by, Mr. Billett—and when you do marry, please send me an invitation—oh I shan't come, I've been far too well brought-up—but I must send—appreciations—and so must have the address. We have had a pleasant acquaintanceship together, haven't we?—perhaps a little more pleasant on my side than on yours—but even so it's *so* nice to think that nothing has ever happened that either of us could really regret.

"Just remember that the only person I could incriminate you to would be Mr. Piper, and not even there very much, due to Sargent's melodramatic appearance in the middle of dinner. But I shan't even there—it would mean incriminating myself a little too much too, don't you know? and even if the apartment here does get a trifle lonely one evening and another, I have got to be extraordinarily fond of it and I couldn't have nearly as nice a one—or as competent an Elizabeth—on what they pay me on 'Mode.' So I'll keep it, I think, if you don't mind.

"But that may make you a little more comfortable when you think things over—and I'm sure we all deserve to be very comfortable indeed for quite a long while after the very trying time we've just been through.

"*Good*-by, and I assure you that even if I shall never be able to think of you in the future except as all wrapped up in the middle of those absurd towels, I shall think of you quite kindly though rather ridiculously nevertheless. And now if you will just run away a minute and wait down in that car of Sargent's that Oliver—borrowed—so effectively—because I must have one motherly word with Oliver alone before we part forever! Thank you so *much*! *Good*-by!"

XLII

So Oliver was left alone with her, he didn't know why. He noticed, however, that when she came to talk to him, though it was still with lightness, she was at no particular effort any longer to make the lightness anything but a method of dealing with wounds.

"Mr. Billett does not seem quite to appreciate exactly how much your timely pugilistics did for him," she observed. "Or exactly how they might have affected you."

Oliver set his jaw, rather. He was hardly going to discuss what Ted might or might not owe him with Mrs. Severance. Hardly.

"No, I suppose you wouldn't," she said uncannily. Then she spoke again and this time if the tone was airy it was with the airiness of a defeated swordsman apologizing for having been killed by such a clumsy stroke of fence.

"But I have some—comprehension—of just what you did. And besides—I seem to have a queer foible for telling the truth just now. Odd, isn't it, when I've been lying so successfully all evening?"

"Very successfully," said Oliver, and, to his astonishment, saw her wince.

"Yes—well. Well, I don't know quite why I'm keeping you

Stephen Vincent Benet

here—though there was something I wanted to say to you, I believe—in a most serious and grandmotherly manner too—the way of a grown woman as Sargent would put it—poor Sargent—" She laughed.

"Oh yes, I remember now. It was only that I don't think you need—worry—about Mr. Billett any more. You see?"

"I think so," said Oliver with some incomprehension.

"Seeing him done up that way in towels," she mused with a flicker of mirth. "And the way he looked at me when I was telling about things afterwards—oh it wouldn't do, you know, Oliver, it wouldn't do! Your friend is—essentially—a—highly—Puritan—young man," she added slowly. Oliver started—that was one of the things so few people knew about Ted.

"Oh yes—wholly. Even in the way he'd go to the devil. He'd do it with such a religious conviction—take it so *hard*. It would eat him up. Completely. And it isn't—amusing—to go to the devil with anybody whose diabolism would be so efficiently pious—a reversed kind of Presbyterianism. We wouldn't do that, you know—you or myself," and for an instant as she spoke Oliver felt what he characterized as a most damnable feeling of kinship with her.

It was true. Oliver had been struck with that during his army experiences—things somehow had never seemed to stick to him the way they had seemed to with Ted.

"Which is one reason that I feel so sure Mr. Billett will get on very well with Sargent's daughter—if his Puritan principles don't make him feel too much as if he were linking her for life to a lost soul," went on Mrs. Severance.

"*Wha-a-at!*"

"My dear Oliver, whatever my failings may be, I have some

penetration. Mr. Billett was garrulous at times, I fear—young men are so apt to be with older women. Oh *no*—he was beautifully sure that he was not betraying himself—the dear ostrich. And that letter—really that was clumsy of both of you, Oliver—when I could see the handwriting—all modern and well-bred girls seem to write the same curly kind of hand somehow—and then Sargent's address in embossed blue letters on the back. And I *couldn't* have suspected him of carrying on an intrigue with Mrs. Piper!" and Oliver was forced to smile at her tinkle of laughter. Then she grew a little earnest.

"I don't suppose it was—Mr. Billett—I wanted so—exactly," she mused. "It was more—Mr. Billett's age—Mr. Billett's undeniable freshness—if you see. I'm not quite a Kipling vampire—no—a vampire that wants to crunch the bones—or do vampires crunch bones? I believe they only act like babies with bottles—nasty of them, isn't it?—But one gets to a definite age—and Sargent's a dear but he has all the defects of a husband—and things begin slipping away, slipping away—"

She made a motion of sifting between her hands, letting fall light grains of a precious substance that the hands were no longer young enough to keep.

"And life goes so queerly and keeps moving on like a tramp in front of a policeman till you've started being gray and taking off your corset every time you're alone because you like being comfortable better than having a waist-line—and you've never had anything to settle you," her face twitched, "not children— nor even the security of marriage—nothing but work that only interests part of you—and this—"

She spread her hands at the apartment.

"Well—what a lot of nonsense I'm talking—and keeping Mr. Billett out in the car when he's sure he has pneumonia already—how unkind of me. You must think me a very immoral old woman, don't you, Oliver?"

"I think you're very sporting," said Oliver, truthfully.

"Not very. If I really *wanted* Mr. Billett, you see." Her eyes sparkled. "I'm afraid you wouldn't think me sporting at all—in that case. But then I don't think you'd have been able to—save—anybody I really wanted as you did Mr. Billett." She spoke slowly. "Even with that very capable looking right hand. But in case you're still worried—"

"I'm not, really."

She paid no attention.

"In case you're still worried—what I told Mr. Billett was true. In the first place, Sargent would never believe me, anyway. In the second place it would mean breaking with Sargent—and do you know I'm rather fond of Sargent in my own way?—and a thing like that—well, you saw how he was tonight—it would mean more things like revolvers and I *hate* revolvers. And hurting Sargent—and ruining Mr. Billett who is a genuinely nice boy and can't help being a Puritan, though I never shall forget the way he looked in those towels. Still, I'm rather fond of him too—oh, I'm perfectly unashamed about it, it's quite in an aunty way now and he'll never see me again if he can help it.

"And making Sargent's daughter—who must be charming from what I hear of her—but charming or not, she happens to be a woman and I have a feeling that, being a woman, life will hurt her quite sufficiently without my adding my wholly vicarious share. Oh, I'm perfectly harmless now, Oliver," she made a pretty gesture with her hands. "You and Sargent and the fire-escape between you have drawn my fangs."

"I can't exactly—thank you," said Oliver, "but I do repeat—you're sporting."

"Never repeat a compliment to a woman over twenty and seldom then." She looked at him reflectively. "The same woman, that is. There is such a great deal I could teach you though, really," she said. "You're much more teachable than Mr. Billett, for instance," and Oliver felt a little shudder of terror go through him for a moment at the way she said it. But she laughed again.

"I shouldn't worry. And besides, you're blighted, aren't you?—and they're unteachable till they recover. Well.

"Oh, yes, there was something else I meant to be serious about. Sargent said something about our—disappearing, and all that. Well, Sargent has always been enamored of puttering around a garden somewhere in an alias and old trousers with me to make him lemonade when he gets overheated—and so far I've humored him—but I've really never thought very much of the idea. That would be—for me—a particularly stupid way of going to seed." She was wholly in earnest now. "And I haven't the slightest intention of going to seed with Sargent or anybody else for a very long time yet. If it ever comes definitely to that I shall break with Sargent; you can depend on my selfishness—arrogance—anything you like for that. Quite depend.

"Tonight," she hesitated. "Tonight has really made a good many things—clear to me. Things that were moving around in my mind, though I didn't know quite what to call them. For one thing, it has made me—realize," her eyes darkened, "that my time for really being—a woman—not in the copybook sense—is diminishing. Getting short. Oh, you and Mr. Billett will have to reconcile your knowledge of Sargent's and my situation with whatever moral ideas you may happen to have on fathers-in-law and friends' fathers for some time yet—I'm sure I don't know how you're going to do it, especially Mr. Billett, and I can't honestly say that I particularly care. But that will not be—permanent, I imagine. You understand?" She put her hand on the door-knob to imply that the audience was over.

"I shall miss Louise, though," she said, frankly.

"Louise will miss you." Oliver saw no need for being politic now. He added hesitatingly, "After all—"

"Oh, no. No," she said lightly but very firmly. "I couldn't very well, now, could I?" and Oliver, in spite of all the broad-mindedness upon which he prided himself, was left rather dumb.

"Oh, it won't be—difficult," she added. "We can keep up—in the office—yes?"

"Yes," said Oliver hastily. He might be signing a compact with all the powers of darkness, but even so.

"For the rest, I am—used to things like that," she added, and once again her face grew suddenly bright with pain. Then she recovered herself.

"Well—our next merry meeting and so forth," she said airily. "Because when it happens, if it does, I may be so stodgily respectable you'll be very glad to ask me to dinner, you know. Or I may be—completely disreputable—one never knows. But in any case," and she gave her hand.

"Mr. Billett must be freezing to death in that car," she murmured. "Good-by, Oliver, and my best if wholly unrespectable good wishes." "Thanks and—good luck to you."

She turned on him swiftly.

"Oh, no. All the happiness in the world and *no* luck—-that's better, isn't it? *Good*-by."

"Good-by."

And then Oliver was out in the hall, pressing the button that would summon a sleepy, disgruntled elevator-boy to take him down to Ted and the car. He decided as he waited that few conversations he had ever had made him feel quite so inescapably, irritatingly young; that he saw to the last inch of exactitude just why Mr. Piper completely and Ted very nearly had fallen in love with Mrs. Severance; that she was one of the most remarkable individuals he had ever met; and that he hoped from the bottom of his heart he never, never saw her again.

XLIII

Ted and he had little conversation going back in the car. The most important part of it occurred when they had left New York behind and were rushing along cool moon-strewn roads to Southampton. Then—

"Thanks," said Ted suddenly and fervently and did not seem to be able to say anything more.

The events of the evening had come too close, at moments, to grotesque tragedy for Oliver to pretend to misunderstand him.

"Oh, that's all right. And anyhow I owed you one for that time with the gendarmes in Brest."

"Maybe," but Ted didn't seem to be convinced. "That was jocose though. Even at the worst." The words came with effort. "This was—serious. I owe you about everything, I guess."

"Oh, go take a flying leap at a galloping goose!"

"Go do it yourself. Oh, Oliver, you ass, I *will* be pretty and polite about your saving my life." And both laughed and felt easier. "Saved a good deal more than that as a matter of fact— or what counts for more with me," Ted added soberly. "Then the letter I brought *was* satisfactory?"

"Satisfactory? Gee!" said Ted intensely, and again they

fell silent.

Some miles later Oliver added casually

"You won't have any trouble with our late hostess, by the way. Though she knows all about it."

"She knows?"

Oliver couldn't resist.

"And quite approves. But she's—a sport." Then for Ted's sake, "Besides, you see, it would crab her game completely."

"I'll tell Elinor, though," said Ted, stubbornly.

"About her father? You can't."

"Oh, Lord, no. About myself. Don't have to give names and addresses."

"Afterwards."

"Well, yes—afterwards. Though it makes me feel like a swine."

"Nobody our age who hasn't been one or felt like one—some of the time—except Christers and the dead," said Oliver, and they proceeded for several minutes on the profundity of that aphorism. The silence was broken by Ted's saying violently,

"I *will* marry her! I don't give a damn what's happened."

"Good egg. Of course you will." Oliver chuckled.

Ted turned to him anxiously after another silence.

"Look Ollie, that bump on my head—you've seen the size it is. Well, is it going to just show up like *thunder* at this silly dance?"

XLIV

Half-past five in the morning and Oliver undressing wearily by the light of a pale pink dawn.

Now and then he looks at his bed with a gloating expression that almost reaches the proportions of a lust—he is so tired he can hardly get off his clothes. The affairs of the last twenty-four hours mix in his mind like a jumble of colored postcards, all loose and disconnected and brightly unreal. Ted—Elinor—Mrs. Severance—Mr. Piper—the dance he has just left—sleep—oh—sleep!

Where is Ted? Somewhere with Elinor of course—it doesn't matter—both were looking suspiciously starry when he last saw them across the room—engagements—marriages—sleep—Mr. Piper's revolver—sleep. How will he return Mr. Piper's revolver? Can't do it tactfully—can't leave it around to be lost, the servants are too efficient—send it to Ted and Elinor as a wedding present—no, that's not tactful either—what silly thoughts—might have been dead by this time—rather better, being alive—and in bed—and asleep—and asleep. Oh, *bed!* and he falls into it as if he were diving into butter and though he murmurs "Nancy" once to himself before his head sinks into pillows, in two seconds he is drugged with such utter slumber that it is only the blind stupefied face of a man under ether that he is able to lift from his haven when Ted comes in half an hour later and announces, in the voice of one proclaiming a new revelation, that Elinor is the finest person that ever lived and that everything is most wholly and completely all right.

XLV

"A letter for you, dear Nancy."

Mrs. Winters gestures at it refinedly—she never points—as Nancy comes in to breakfast looking as if whatever sleep she had had not done her very much good.

"From your dear, dear mother, I should imagine," she adds in sugared watery tones.

Nancy opens it without much interest—Mother, oh, yes, Mother. Six crossed pages of St. Louis gossip and wanderingly fluent advice. She sets herself to read it, though, dutifully enough—she is under Mrs. Winters' eyes.

Father's usual September cold. The evil ways of friends' servants. Good wishes to Mrs. Winters. "Heart's Gold—such a really *inspiring* moving-picture." Advice. Advice. Then, half-way down the next to last page Nancy stops puzzledly. She doesn't quite understand.

"And hope, my daughter, that now you are really cured though you may have passed through bitter waters but all such things are but God's divine will to chasten us. And when the young man told me of his *escapade* I felt that even over the telephone he might have"

She sets herself wearily to decode some sort of definite meaning out of Mother's elliptic style. An escapade. Of Oliver?

and over the telephone—what was that? Mother hadn't said anything—

She finishes the letter and then rereads all the parts of it that seem to have any bearing on the cryptogram, and finally near the end, and evidently connected with the "telephone," she comes upon the phrase "that day."

There is only one day that Mother alludes to as "That Day" now. Before her broken engagement "That Day" was when Father failed.

But Oliver *hadn't* telephoned—she'd asked Mother *particularly* if he had, and he hadn't. But surely if he had telephoned, surely, surely, Mother would have told her about it—Mother would have known that there were a few things where she really hadn't any right to interfere.

Mother had never liked Oliver, though she'd pretended. Never.

Nancy remembers back and with fatally clear vision. It is fortunate that Mrs. Ellicott cannot turn over with Nancy that little shelf-full of memories—all the small places where she was not quite truthful with Nancy, where she was not quite fair, where she "kept things from her"—Mrs. Ellicott has always been the kind of woman who believes in "keeping things from" people as long as possible and then "breaking them gently." Almost any sort of things.

It is still more fortunate that Mrs. Ellicott cannot see Nancy's eyes as she reviews all the tiny deceptions, all the petty affairs about which she was never told or trusted—and all for her own best interests, my dear, Mrs. Ellicott would most believingly assure her—but when parents stand so much in Loco Dei to nearly all children—and when the children have long ago found out that their God is not only a jealous God but one that must be wheedled and propitiated like an early Jehovah because that is the only thing to be done with Gods you can't trust—

Nancy doesn't *want* to believe. She keeps telling herself that she won't, she absolutely won't unless she absolutely has to. But she is lucky or unlucky enough to be a person of some intuition—she knows Oliver, and, also, she knows her mother—though now she is beginning to think with an empty feeling that she really doesn't know the latter at all.

What facts there are are rather like Mrs. Ellicott's handwriting—vague and crossed and illegibly hard to read. But Nancy stares at them all the time that she is eating her breakfast and responding mechanically to Mrs. Winters' questions. And then, suddenly, she *knows*.

Mrs. Ellicott like many inexperienced criminals, has committed the deadly error of letting her mind dwell too long on the *mise-en-scene* of her crime. And her pen—that tell-tale pen that all her life she has taken a delight almost sensual in letting run on from unwieldy sentence to pious formless sentence, has at last betrayed her completely. There is genuine tragedy in store for Mrs. Ellicott—Nancy in spite of being modern, is Nancy and will forgive her—but Nancy, for all her trying, will never quite be able to respect her again.

Nancy doesn't finish her breakfast as neatly as Mrs. Winters would have wished. She goes into the next room to telephone.

"Business, dear?" says Mrs. Winters brightly from the midst of a last piece of toast and "Yes—something Mother wants me to do" from Nancy, unfairly.

Then she gives the number—it is still the same number she and Oliver used when they used to talk after he had caught the last train back to Melgrove and both by all principles that make for the Life Efficient should have gone to bed—though to Nancy's mind that seems a great while ago. "Can I speak to Mrs. Crowe, please?" The explaining can be as awful as it likes, Nancy doesn't care any more. An agitated rustle comes to her ears—that must be Mrs. Winters listening.

"Mrs. Crowe? This—is—Nancy—Ellicott."

She says it very loudly and distinctly and for Mrs. Winters to hear.

XLVI

Oliver wakes around one o'clock with a dim consciousness that noisy crowds of people have been talking very loudly at him a good many too many times during the past few hours, but that he has managed to fool them, many or few, by always acting as much like a Body as possible. His chief wish is to turn over on the other side and sleep for another seven hours or so, but one of those people is standing respectfully beside his bed and though Oliver blinks eyes at him reproachfully, he will not vanish back into his proper nonentity—he remains standing there—obsequious words come out of his mouth.

"Ten minutes to one, sir. Lunch is at one, sir."

Oliver stares at the blue waistcoat gloomily. "What's that?"

"Ten minutes to one, sir. Lunch is at one, sir."

"Lunch?"

"Yes, sir."

"Then I'd better get up, I suppose. Ow-*ooh!*" as he stretches.

"Yes, sir. A bath, sir?" "Bath?"

"Yes, sir."

"Oh, yes, bath. No—don't bother—I mean, I'll take it myself.

You needn't watch me."

"Certainly *not*, sir. Thank you, sir. There have been several telephone calls for you, sir."

Oliver sighs—he is really awake now—it will be less trouble to get up than to try and go back to sleep. Besides, if he tries, that brass-buttoned automaton in front of him will probably start shaking him gently in its well-trained English way.

"Telephone calls? Who telephone-called?"

"The name was Crowe, sir. The lady who was calling said she would call again around lunch time. She said you were to be sure to wait until she called, sir."

"Oh, yes, certainly." Politely, "And now I think I'll get up, if you don't mind?"

"Oh, no, sir," rather scandalizedly. "You are in need of nothing, sir?"

Oliver thinks of replying, "Oh, just bring me a little more sleep if you have it in the house," but then thinks better of it.

"No, thanks."

"Very good, sir," and the automaton pussyfoots away.

Oliver still half asleep manages to rise and find slippers and a wrapper and then pads over to an empty bathroom where he disports himself like a whale. To his surprise he discovers himself whistling—true, the sunlight has an excellent shine to it this morning and the air and the sky outside seem blue and crisp with first fall—but even so.

"Nancy," he murmurs and frowns and finishes his bath rather gloomily—a gloom which is in no wise diminished when he goes downstairs to find everybody nearly through lunch and

Ted and Elinor, as far away from each other at the table as possible, quite sure that they are behaving exactly as usual while the remnants of the house-party do their best to seem tactfully unconcerned.

Oliver, while managing to get through a copious and excellent lunch in spite of his sorrows, regards them with the morose pity of a dyspeptic octogenarian for healthy children. It is all very well and beautiful for them now, he supposes grimly, but sooner or later even such babes as they will have to Face Life— Come Up Against Facts—

He is having a second piece of blueberry pie when he is summoned to the telephone. Rather tiresome of Mother, really, he thinks as he goes out of the dining-room— something about his laundry again most probably—or when he is coming back.

"Hello, Oliver?" "Hello, dear. Anything important?"

Mrs. Crowe's voice has a tiny chuckle in it—a chuckle that only comes when Mrs. Crowe is being very pleased indeed.

"Well, Oliver, that depends—"

"Well, Mother, *honestly*! I'm right in the middle of lunch—"

"Oh, I'll call up again, if you'd rather, Oliver dear." But Mrs. Crowe for private reasons doesn't seem to be at all ashamed of taking up so much of her son's very valuable time.

"Only I *did* think it would interest you—that you'd like to know as soon as possible."

Impatiently, "Yes. Well?"

"Well—a friend of yours is coming to see you on the three o'clock. A *rather* good friend. We thought you'd be back by then, you see, and so—"

Oliver's heart jumps queerly for an instant.

"*Who?*"

But the imp of the perverse has taken complete charge of Mrs. Crowe.

"Oh—a friend. Not a childhood one—oh, no—but a—good—one, though you haven't seen each other for—more than three weeks now, isn't it? You should just be able to make it, I should think, if somebody brought you over in a car, but of course, if you're so busy—" "*Mother!*"

Then Oliver jangles the little hook of the telephone frantically up and down.

"Mother! Listen! Listen! Who is it? Is it—honestly?"

But Mrs. Crowe has hung up. Shall he get the connection again? But that means waiting—and Mother said he would just be able to make it—and Mother isn't at all the kind that would fool him over a thing like this no matter how much she wanted to tease. Oliver bounds back toward the dining-room and nearly runs into Elinor Piper. He grabs her by the shoulders.

"Listen, El!" he says feverishly. "Oh, I'll congratulate you properly and all that some time but this is utterly everything—I've got to go home right away—this minute—toot sweet—and no, by gum, I won't apologize *this* time for asking you to get somebody to take me over in a car!"

Stephen Vincent Benet

XLVII

She was sitting on the porch of the house—a small figure in the close blue hat he knew, a figure that seemed as if it had come tired from a long journey. She had been talking with his mother, but as soon as the car drew up, Mrs. Crowe rose quickly and went into the house.

Then they were together again.

The instant paid them for all. For the last weeks' bitterness and the human doubt, the human misunderstandings that had made it. And even as it opened before them a path some corners and resting-places of which seemed almost too proud with living for them to dare to be alive on it—both knew that that fidelity which is intense and of the soul had ended between them forever an emptier arrogance that both had once delighted in like bright colors—a brittle pride that lives only by the falser things in being young.

They had thought they were sure of each other in their first weeks together—they had said many words about it and some of them clever enough. But their surety now had no need of any words at all—it had been too well tempered by desolation to find any obligation for speech or the calling of itself secure.

They kissed—not as a pleasant gesture, and no fear of looking publicly ridiculous stopped them.

The screen door behind Nancy pushed open. Jane Ellen

appeared, Jane Ellen, by the look of her, intent upon secret and doubtful business, a large moth-eaten bear dangling by its leg from one of her plump hands. She was too concerned with getting her charge through the door to notice what was happening at first but as soon as she was fairly out on the porch she looked about her. The bear dropped from her fingers—her eyes grew rounder than buttons and very large.

"Why it's Oliver and he's kissing Aunt *Nancy*!" she squeaked in a small voice of reproachful surprise.

XLVIII

Whatever the number was of the second-class stateroom on the *Citric*, it was rather too far down in the belly of that leviathan to have suited fashionable people. But Oliver and Nancy had stopped being fashionable some time before and they told each other that it was *much* nicer than first-class on one of the small liners with apparent conviction and never got tired of rejoicing at their luck in its being an outside. It was true that the port-hole might most of the time have been wholly ornamental for all the good it did them, for it was generally splashed with grey October sea, but, at least, as Nancy lucently explained, you could see things—once there had actually been a porpoise—and that neither of them, in their present condition, would have worried very much about it if their cabin had been an aquarium was a fact beyond dispute.

"Time to get up, dear!" This is Oliver a little sternly from the upper berth. "That was your bath that came in a minute ago and said something in Cockney. At least I *think* it was—mine's voice is a good deal more like one of Peter's butlers—" "But, Ollie, I'm so *comfortable!*"

"So am I. But think of breakfast."

"Well—breakfast is a point." Then she chuckles, "Oh, Ollie, wouldn't it have been *awful* if we'd either of us been bad sailors!"

"We couldn't have been," says Oliver placidly. "We have too

much luck."

"I know but—that awful woman with the face like a green pea—oh, Ollie, you'd have hated me—we are lucky, darling."

Oliver has thought seriously enough about getting up to be dangling his legs over the edge of his shelf by now.

"Aren't we?" he says soberly. "I mean I am."

"*I* am. And everybody's being so nice about giving us checks we can use instead of a lot of silly things we wouldn't know what to do with." She smiles. "Those are your feet," she announces gravely.

"Yes. Well?"

"Oh, nothing. Only I'm going to tickle them."

"You're not? Ouch—Nancy, you *little devil*." and Oliver slides hastily to the floor. Then he goes over to the port-hole.

"A very nice day!" he announces in the face of a bull's eye view of dull skies and oily dripping sea.

"Is it? How kind of it! Ollie, I must get up." "Nancy, you must." He goes over and kneels awkwardly by the side of her berth—an absurd figure enough no doubt in tortoise-shell spectacles and striped pajamas, but Nancy doesn't think so. As for him he simply knows he never will get used to having her with him this way all the time; he takes his breath delicately whenever he thinks of it, as if, if he weren't very careful always about being quiet she might disappear any instant like a fairy back into a book.

He kisses her.

"Good morning, Nancy."

Her arms go round him.

"Good morning, dearest."

"It isn't that I don't want to get up, really," she explains presently. "It's only that I like lying here and thinking about all the things that are going to happen."

"We are lucky, you know. Lordy bless the American Express."

"And my job." She smiles and he winces.

"Oh, Ollie, *dear.*"

"I was so damn silly," says Oliver muffledly.

"Both of us. But now it doesn't matter. And we're both of us going to work and be very efficient at it—only now we'll have time and together and Paris to do all the things we really wanted to do. You *are* going to be a great novelist, Oliver, you know—"

"Well, you're going to be the foremost etcher—or etcheress—since Whistler—there. But, oh, Nancy, I don't care if I write great novels—or any novels—or anything else—just now."

She mocks him pleasantly. "Why, Ollie, Ollie, Your Art?"

"Oh, *damn* my art—I mean—well, I don't quite mean that. But this is life."

"Just as large and twice as natural," says Nancy quoting, but for once Oliver is too interested with living to be literary.

"Life," he says, with an odd shakiness, an odd triumph, "Life," and his arms go round her shoulders.

ABOUT THE AUTHOR

Stephen Vincent Benét (July 22, 1898, Fountain Hill, Pennsylvania, United States–March 13, 1943) was an American author, poet, short story writer and novelist. He is best known for his narrative poem of the American Civil War, John Brown's Body, published in 1928. He won a Pulitzer Prize for this work in 1929.

Benet's fantasy short story "The Devil and Daniel Webster" won an O. Henry Award, and he furnished the material for a one-act opera by Douglas Moore.

Benét was born into an Army family in Fountain Hill, Pennsylvania, near Bethlehem in Pennsylvania's Lehigh Valley. He spent most of his boyhood in Benicia, California. At the age of about ten, Benét was sent to the Hitchcock Military Academy. A graduate of The Albany Academy in Albany, New York and Yale University, he was awarded a posthumous Pulitzer Prize in 1944 for "Western Star", an unfinished narrative poem on the settling of America.

It was a line of Benet's poetry that gave the title to Dee Brown's famous history of the destruction of Native American tribes by the United States: Bury My Heart at Wounded Knee.

Benet's brother, William Rose Benét (1886–1950), was a poet, anthologist and critic who is largely remembered for his desk reference, The Reader's Cyclopedia (1948).

Choose from Thousands of 1stWorldLibrary Classics By

A. M. Barnard
Ada Leverson
Adolphus William Ward
Aesop
Agatha Christie
Alexander Aaronsohn
Alexander Kielland
Alexandre Dumas
Alfred Gatty
Alfred Ollivant
Alice Duer Miller
Alice Turner Curtis
Alice Dunbar
Allen Chapman
Alleyne Ireland
Ambrose Bierce
Amelia E. Barr
Amory H. Bradford
Andrew Lang
Andrew McFarland Davis
Andy Adams
Angela Brazil
Anna Alice Chapin
Anna Sewell
Annie Besant
Annie Hamilton Donnell
Annie Payson Call
Annie Roe Carr
Annonaymous
Anton Chekhov
Archibald Lee Fletcher
Arnold Bennett
Arthur C. Benson
Arthur Conan Doyle
Arthur M. Winfield
Arthur Ransome
Arthur Schnitzler
Arthur Train
Atticus
B.H. Baden-Powell
B. M. Bower
B. C. Chatterjee
Baroness Emmuska Orczy
Baroness Orczy
Basil King
Bayard Taylor
Ben Macomber
Bertha Muzzy Bower
Bjornstjerne Bjornson

Booth Tarkington
Boyd Cable
Bram Stoker
C. Collodi
C. E. Orr
C. M. Ingleby
Carolyn Wells
Catherine Parr Traill
Charles A. Eastman
Charles Amory Beach
Charles Dickens
Charles Dudley Warner
Charles Farrar Browne
Charles Ives
Charles Kingsley
Charles Klein
Charles Hanson Towne
Charles Lathrop Pack
Charles Romyn Dake
Charles Whibley
Charles Willing Beale
Charlotte M. Braeme
Charlotte M. Yonge
Charlotte Perkins Stetson
Clair W. Hayes
Clarence Day Jr.
Clarence E. Mulford
Clemence Housman
Confucius
Coningsby Dawson
Cornelis DeWitt Wilcox
Cyril Burleigh
D. H. Lawrence
Daniel Defoe
David Garnett
Dinah Craik
Don Carlos Janes
Donald Keyhoe
Dorothy Kilner
Dougan Clark
Douglas Fairbanks
E. Nesbit
E. P. Roe
E. Phillips Oppenheim
E. S. Brooks
Earl Barnes
Edgar Rice Burroughs
Edith Van Dyne
Edith Wharton

Edward Everett Hale
Edward J. O'Biren
Edward S. Ellis
Edwin L. Arnold
Eleanor Atkins
Eleanor Hallowell Abbott
Eliot Gregory
Elizabeth Gaskell
Elizabeth McCracken
Elizabeth Von Arnim
Ellem Key
Emerson Hough
Emilie F. Carlen
Emily Bronte
Emily Dickinson
Enid Bagnold
Enilor Macartney Lane
Erasmus W. Jones
Ernie Howard Pie
Ethel May Dell
Ethel Turner
Ethel Watts Mumford
Eugene Sue
Eugenie Foa
Eugene Wood
Eustace Hale Ball
Evelyn Everett-green
Everard Cotes
F. H. Cheley
F. J. Cross
F. Marion Crawford
Fannie E. Newberry
Federick Austin Ogg
Ferdinand Ossendowski
Fergus Hume
Florence A. Kilpatrick
Fremont B. Deering
Francis Bacon
Francis Darwin
Frances Hodgson Burnett
Frances Parkinson Keyes
Frank Gee Patchin
Frank Harris
Frank Jewett Mather
Frank L. Packard
Frank V. Webster
Frederic Stewart Isham
Frederick Trevor Hill
Frederick Winslow Taylor

Friedrich Kerst
Friedrich Nietzsche
Fyodor Dostoyevsky
G.A. Henty
G.K. Chesterton
Gabrielle E. Jackson
Garrett P. Serviss
Gaston Leroux
George A. Warren
George Ade
Geroge Bernard Shaw
George Cary Eggleston
George Durston
George Ebers
George Eliot
George Gissing
George MacDonald
George Meredith
George Orwell
George Sylvester Viereck
George Tucker
George W. Cable
George Wharton James
Gertrude Atherton
Gordon Casserly
Grace E. King
Grace Gallatin
Grace Greenwood
Grant Allen
Guillermo A. Sherwell
Gulielma Zollinger
Gustav Flaubert
H. A. Cody
H. B. Irving
H.C. Bailey
H. G. Wells
H. H. Munro
H. Irving Hancock
H. R. Naylor
H. Rider Haggard
H. W. C. Davis
Haldeman Julius
Hall Caine
Hamilton Wright Mabie
Hans Christian Andersen
Harold Avery
Harold McGrath
Harriet Beecher Stowe
Harry Castlemon
Harry Coghill
Harry Houidini

Hayden Carruth
Helent Hunt Jackson
Helen Nicolay
Hendrik Conscience
Hendy David Thoreau
Henri Barbusse
Henrik Ibsen
Henry Adams
Henry Ford
Henry Frost
Henry James
Henry Jones Ford
Henry Seton Merriman
Henry W Longfellow
Herbert A. Giles
Herbert Carter
Herbert N. Casson
Herman Hesse
Hildegard G. Frey
Homer
Honore De Balzac
Horace B. Day
Horace Walpole
Horatio Alger Jr.
Howard Pyle
Howard R. Garis
Hugh Lofting
Hugh Walpole
Humphry Ward
Ian Maclaren
Inez Haynes Gillmore
Irving Bacheller
Isabel Cecilia Williams
Isabel Hornibrook
Israel Abrahams
Ivan Turgenev
J.G.Austin
J. Henri Fabre
J. M. Barrie
J. M. Walsh
J. Macdonald Oxley
J. R. Miller
J. S. Fletcher
J. S. Knowles
J. Storer Clouston
J. W. Duffield
Jack London
Jacob Abbott
James Allen
James Andrews
James Baldwin

James Branch Cabell
James DeMille
James Joyce
James Lane Allen
James Lane Allen
James Oliver Curwood
James Oppenheim
James Otis
James R. Driscoll
Jane Abbott
Jane Austen
Jane L. Stewart
Janet Aldridge
Jens Peter Jacobsen
Jerome K. Jerome
Jessie Graham Flower
John Buchan
John Burroughs
John Cournos
John F. Kennedy
John Gay
John Glasworthy
John Habberton
John Joy Bell
John Kendrick Bangs
John Milton
John Philip Sousa
John Taintor Foote
Jonas Lauritz Idemil Lie
Jonathan Swift
Joseph A. Altsheler
Joseph Carey
Joseph Conrad
Joseph E. Badger Jr
Joseph Hergesheimer
Joseph Jacobs
Jules Vernes
Julian Hawthrone
Julie A Lippmann
Justin Huntly McCarthy
Kakuzo Okakura
Karle Wilson Baker
Kate Chopin
Kenneth Grahame
Kenneth McGaffey
Kate Langley Bosher
Kate Langley Bosher
Katherine Cecil Thurston
Katherine Stokes
L. A. Abbot
L. T. Meade

L. Frank Baum
Latta Griswold
Laura Dent Crane
Laura Lee Hope
Laurence Housman
Lawrence Beasley
Leo Tolstoy
Leonid Andreyev
Lewis Carroll
Lewis Sperry Chafer
Lilian Bell
Lloyd Osbourne
Louis Hughes
Louis Joseph Vance
Louis Tracy
Louisa May Alcott
Lucy Fitch Perkins
Lucy Maud Montgomery
Luther Benson
Lydia Miller Middleton
Lyndon Orr
M. Corvus
M. H. Adams
Margaret E. Sangster
Margret Howth
Margaret Vandercook
Margaret W. Hungerford
Margret Penrose
Maria Edgeworth
Maria Thompson Daviess
Mariano Azuela
Marion Polk Angellotti
Mark Overton
Mark Twain
Mary Austin
Mary Catherine Crowley
Mary Cole
Mary Hastings Bradley
Mary Roberts Rinehart
Mary Rowlandson
M. Wollstonecraft Shelley
Maud Lindsay
Max Beerbohm
Myra Kelly
Nathaniel Hawthrone
Nicolo Machiavelli
O. F. Walton
Oscar Wilde
Owen Johnson
P.G. Wodehouse
Paul and Mabel Thorne

Paul G. Tomlinson
Paul Severing
Percy Brebner
Percy Keese Fitzhugh
Peter B. Kyne
Plato
Quincy Allen
R. Derby Holmes
R. L. Stevenson
R. S. Ball
Rabindranath Tagore
Rahul Alvares
Ralph Bonehill
Ralph Henry Barbour
Ralph Victor
Ralph Waldo Emmerson
Rene Descartes
Ray Cummings
Rex Beach
Rex E. Beach
Richard Harding Davis
Richard Jefferies
Richard Le Gallienne
Robert Barr
Robert Frost
Robert Gordon Anderson
Robert L. Drake
Robert Lansing
Robert Lynd
Robert Michael Ballantyne
Robert W. Chambers
Rosa Nouchette Carey
Rudyard Kipling
Saint Augustine
Samuel B. Allison
Samuel Hopkins Adams
Sarah Bernhardt
Sarah C. Hallowell
Selma Lagerlof
Sherwood Anderson
Sigmund Freud
Standish O'Grady
Stanley Weyman
Stella Benson
Stella M. Francis
Stephen Crane
Stewart Edward White
Stijn Streuvels
Swami Abhedananda
Swami Parmananda
T. S. Ackland

T. S. Arthur
The Princess Der Ling
Thomas A. Janvier
Thomas A Kempis
Thomas Anderton
Thomas Bailey Aldrich
Thomas Bulfinch
Thomas De Quincey
Thomas Dixon
Thomas H. Huxley
Thomas Hardy
Thomas More
Thornton W. Burgess
U. S. Grant
Upton Sinclair
Valentine Williams
Various Authors
Vaughan Kester
Victor Appleton
Victor G. Durham
Victoria Cross
Virginia Woolf
Wadsworth Camp
Walter Camp
Walter Scott
Washington Irving
Wilbur Lawton
Wilkie Collins
Willa Cather
Willard F. Baker
William Dean Howells
William le Queux
W. Makepeace Thackeray
William W. Walter
William Shakespeare
Winston Churchill
Yei Theodora Ozaki
Yogi Ramacharaka
Young E. Allison
Zane Grey

www.ingramcontent.com/pod-product-compliance
Lightning Source LLC
Chambersburg PA
CBHW050036180626
46810CB00002B/736